LAND OF THE FREE... NEGROES

DARYL CUMBER DANCE
A HISTORICAL NOVEL

A FICTION IMPRINT FROM ADDUCENT

LAND OF THE FREE... NEGROES

DARYL CUMBER DANCE
A HISTORICAL NOVEL

LAND OF THE FREE... NEGROES

Daryl Cumber Dance

ISBN (paperback) 9781937592943

Published by YORE (A Historical Fiction Imprint from Adducent)
www.AdducentCreative.com
Jacksonville, Florida USA
Published in the United States of America

Cover Illustration Copyright © 2020 by Adducent, Inc.
Cover, Book Design and Production by Adducent.

This is a work of fiction, but most of the characters are historical figures. Their actions and dialogue are fictionalized by the author. While a few actual events and settings are depicted, most are not, and story details, including plot, have been fictionalized.

ADVANCE PRAISE

In *Land of the Free*, Daryl Dance vividly brings to life Charles City, Virginia's rich and complex history through her fictional depiction of the Browns, an antebellum family of free people of color who bear freedom's steep cost with courage, ingenuity, and cunning, but "not without laughter." Dance has extensively drawn from the extraordinary experiences of her own ancestors, skillfully rendering their actions within the context of their times. These are people Dance knows intimately; they not only subsisted under the morally bankrupt institution of slavery, but finally prevailed through their love for each other and their abiding Christian faith. This is a must-read for students of early American history interested in the seldom-told story of how "we got over."

> -Hermine Pinson, Margaret Hamilton Professor of
> English & Africana Studies, William & Mary

Daryl Dance's *Land of the Free... Negroes*, is a masterful mesh of family history, significant research, and poetic literary imagination. She uses the literal truth of names, places, and circumstances and broadens the specific into a picture of a whole society, as wild and as real as her British forebear, named Moll, borrowed from Daniel Defoe's Moll Flanders. This mix is a feat to be admired and a feast for the reader. The plot traces stories and events in the lineage of a family of free Blacks in Charles City, Virginia, during the 18th and 19th centuries. From the moment in 1743 when Elizabeth, free, white, and now coupled with John, free and Black, is forcibly deprived of her two mixed sons to be indentured by the power of their white father, the novella sets forth its twisting threads. The violence of this loss propels the story through generations. I love this book for the tension that quickens heart and breath at each development. That free Negroes, those never enslaved, are burdened in the era of slavery by risks grounded in their very freedom is a revealing paradox. Here find kidnapping, revenge, mob justice, spiritual vision, inspiration, mystery, love, and magic-made-real all in the service of triumphant family survival.

-Mary Moore Easter, poet, *The Body of the World*

TABLE OF CONTENTS

ACKNOWLEDGMENTS

This book was conceived and written so long ago that I don't even remember all who may have helped me during its composition. I began work on this when I was working on another project in 1998-99 as a resident fellow in The Center for Advanced Study in the Behavioral Sciences in Stanford, CA. For a change of pace, I registered for a community creative writing class, with whom I shared the first couple of chapters. I thank my teacher, Barbara Noble, and my classmates, none of whose names I recall, for their encouraging responses and suggestions as I began to write the first two chapters.

I also thank Joanne Gabbin and Ethel Morgan Smith, two of my Wintergreen sisters, who critiqued the opening two chapters of this novel in 1999.

I am indebted to Daniel Defoe for creating such a fascinating character in *The Fortunes and Misfortunes of the Famous Moll Flanders Who was born in Newgate, and during a life of continu'd Variety for Threescore Years, besides her Childhood, was Twelve Years a Whore, five times a Wife (whereof once to her brother) Twelve Years a Thief, Eight Years a Transported Felon in Virginia, at last grew Rich, liv'd Honest and died a Penitent* that I decided to borrow her and make her a character in my novel.

My thanks to The Center for Advanced Study in the Behavioral Sciences in Stanford, CA, for the opportunity to spend 1998-99 in residence there.

I am also indebted to the Stanford University Libraries for allowing me full use of their facilities during my residency.

I am grateful to Dennis Lowery and his company, Adducent, for the excellent work in editing, formatting, and designing this book.

INTRODUCTION

As I was completing my family genealogy, *The Lineage of Abraham: the History of a Free Black Family in Charles City, VA*, in 1998, I continued to feel frustrated that I had been unable to tell the complete stories of some of those remarkable ancestors whom I had treated. Finally, I decided that if I could not further document their lives, I would fictionalize their stories. I immediately started work on this project, *Land of the Free... Negroes*, but it found its way to my bookshelves as I turned my attention to a study of Jamaica Kincaid and then had to deal with my husband's illness and death. Ultimately, my daughter and I updated and reprinted *The Lineage of Abraham* in 2020.

The pandemic of 2020 offered me the time and opportunity to dust off a couple of writing projects that had been gathering dust for several years, including *Land of the Free... Negroes*.

The major characters in this novel (Elizabeth, Abraham, Will, John, Susannah, and Polly Brown) are based on actual historical figures by the same names; other characters, like James Seldorn, William Joseph Danzee, and Josh, are completely or almost-completely fictional. Moll is borrowed from Daniel Defoe, some of whose adventures lent themselves to my story, so I adapted her and created a completely fictional role for her in my family.

Much of the plot in this novel is completely fictional. Having exhausted all the documents available to me, having consulted all the historical accounts I could trust, having accepted the fact that there were no sources that could reveal the basic realities of my ancestors' inner lives, I turned within and arrived at the same realization that sparked Zora Neale Hurston:

> Like the dead-seeming cold rocks, I have memories within that came out of the material that went to make me. Time and place have had their say. - *Dust Tracks on a Road*

Emboldened, I set out on the same archeological journey that Toni Morrison describes:

> "On the basis of some information and a little bit of guesswork, you journey to a site to see what remains were left behind and to reconstruct the world that these remains imply." - *The Site of Memory*

Turning to my "memories within" and my extended genealogical study of my ancestors' history, I allowed myself the freedom to delve into their memories, to reconstruct their lives, to discern their emotions, to reimagine their words, and to create and preserve for their descendants a close and intimate look into the complex inner lives of those who peopled *The Land of the Free... Negroes*.

MY DEBT TO THE ANCESTORS

I have spent a life listening to the tales of old people,
Searching through birth and death certificates, tax rolls
and voting records,
Poring over free papers, wills, and land transfers,
Reading trial records and Civil War claims,
Handling dusty books and turning crumbling pages,
Staring back at oversized pictures of ancients glaring
down at me from a wall,
And sassy Flappers winking at me from the pages of a
scrapbook.

I have spent the last twenty years cutting and pasting,
Putting together scraps of memorates and court records
and haunting pictures,
Trying to create a collage of the ancestors--to make them
whole.

But they seem unhappy with my collage,
I sense they do not consider it authentic.
They were not some pasted re-creation of bits and pieces,
some puzzle with visible cracks and missing parts.
They were real, whole, three-dimensional, living,
breathing, suffering, laughing individuals.
They want to be remembered as they were.
So now, doubly unhappy, they scowl at me from their
pictures on the wall.

I write and write, sweat and labor, look up at those
pictures still demanding more.

I am tired of enduring their pains and suffering, their
humiliations and defeats,
I am tired even of celebrating their victories and detailing
their achievements.
I twist and turn, move from one side of the room to the other,
But accusing eyes follow me everywhere;
It does not help to turn away from their gaze, to leave the
room,
Even to gather up my notes and flee to Charlottesville, to
California.
Even in those distant places voices of shadows whisper in
my ear,
Insisting that I have yet more to do.

"What do you want of me?" I plead.
"You are ghosts I do not know and have never seen.
I have followed you from gravestones to distant cities and
obscure archives,
I have walked with you down country roads and
university paths, even trailed you to bloody battle fields.
I have waked, breathed, slept, and dreamed with you all
these years.
I have a life to lead, let me be!"

And then finally an epiphany--
I cannot write about them.
Two self-contained individuals, one creating another.
We are not separate beings--they, the historical
characters, and I, the objective scholar.
No, the Ancestors are me and I am them
And this is not my telling of their story;
This is my effort to tell our story.

-Daryl Cumber Dance

Open your ears to the ancestors, and you will understand the language of spirits.

AFRICAN PROVERB

CHAPTER ONE

THE INDENTURE OF ABRAHAM AND JOHN

Those white things have taken all I had or dreamed... and broke my heartstrings too. There is no bad luck in the world but white folks.

-Baby Suggs, in Toni Morrison, *Beloved*

Later Elizabeth would find one thing to be happy about that accursed day—James was not home. He almost certainly would have tried to stop them from taking her boys, and he would have been arrested and jailed, or maybe even killed.

It was shad season, and he had set off for Josh's house at 5 a.m. with her youngest son, Will. He was going to drop Will off to spend the day with Josh's children while the two brothers went fishing on the James River.

Elizabeth was working with her sons John and Abraham on their writing lessons when suddenly their attention was arrested by a tragic scene erupting in their front yard.

A baby bird had fallen out of the nest and was frantically scrambling on the ground, too undeveloped to walk or even stand. The mother bird flew wildly around, diving down to her chick, circling her, unable to decide upon the proper course of action. Three other chicks stared down from their nest.

Out on the road in front of the house, Elizabeth glimpsed two horsemen. She was mildly surprised when they turned in at her gate. Though there was a gradual sense of discomfort, she did not anticipate that their visit would be anything alarming. They tied their horses to a post in her front yard, and the tallest one snatched a piece of paper out of his saddlebag. She stepped off her porch and greeted her unexpected guests in a trembling voice: "Morning, gentlem…"

"We've come for John and Abraham Brown," they coldly announced, handing her the court order from the March 1743 Court of Charles City County, Virginia, that they didn't expect she could read:

Ordered that the two children of Elizabeth Brown (namely) John & Abraham be bound by the churchwardens to William Joseph Danzee as the law directs.

"But my children are free. My mother was a White Englishwoman. We have never been slaves," she protested, confident that this must be some mistake.

"The c-c-court has ordered that the t-t-two children of Elizabeth--" the short one began reading, not sure she had comprehended the court order.

"We not here to discuss the court order with you, but to deliver the children to Mr. Danzee as directed," the tall one interrupted. "This don't mean they're slaves. This means the court determined your base-born children shouldn't continue here with you living in sin with that free nigger. Mr. Danzee has already executed the indenture papers, and we here to take the children to him."

The boys clutched her skirt. She hugged them to her.

"Please-e-e, don't take my children, I beg you. Lord Jesus Christ, don't take my children! James and I gon' get married. Please just give me a little time."

"Just get any clothes you want those lil niggers to take with them," the tall one continued. "We ain't here to argue with you. We here to execute the court's orders. You got a right to appeal if you want to, but for the time being, we have to take them with us."

"Appeal?... Where?... How?... Can't you wait for me to get this mistake straightened out? Abraham's got a cold, and John's got a bad infection on his toe I'm working on. They can't leave home now—you hear me!" she started screaming now that the men were grabbing the frightened, whimpering boys from her grasp and throwing them up on the horses. As she continued to desperately try to pull first one and then the other back to her, the tall man struck her a debilitating blow with his whip, shredding the back of her dress and knocking her to her knees. Then whacking the whip across the horse's backsides, he yelled, "Gittup!" And they were off, leaving her in the unsettled dust.

The loud, long scream erupting from the frenzied mother's convulsive breast was echoed by the equally vociferous squawks of the bird, now trying to fight off a fat white cat that seemed determined to snatch her chick. The mother bird flew down at the cat, wildly flapping her wings and pecking at him. But the hard-hearted stalker, though distracted, was not to be deterred.

Elizabeth rushed over, kicked the cat away, and, pulling her apron over her head lest the mother bird attack her, picked up the trembling chick. The mother bird circled overhead but did not move toward Elizabeth, evidently grateful that she, and not the malevolent cat, held her offspring. Elizabeth climbed on James' conveniently

3

placed carriage and reached up to tenderly lay her charge in its mother's nest. The mother bird circled calmly until Elizabeth had climbed down to the ground. Then, relieved, she flew to rejoin her restored family.

Elizabeth dragged herself into her empty house.

News spread quickly through the little Negro community of Freetown, and by nightfall, Elizabeth and James' modest cottage was filled with chattering neighbors. Many were not at all surprised. It was common knowledge those White plantation owners grabbed every little illegitimate colored child they could to get more free labor for their plantations—even if their mothers were *White*. Many of the women said Elizabeth was lucky she got to keep her children this long—after all, Abraham was eight and John was seven. Apparently, no one in the Negro community except Elizabeth was surprised at this turn of events.

Elizabeth, comfortable in the protection of her long-ago disappeared White British mother and her long-dead free Indian and African father never dreamed that she would ever experience what she had witnessed around her all of her life—mothers shrieking as their children were taken away from them.

"You lucky," one of her neighbors consoled: "they ain't taken as slaves and they with their father, not moren five miles down the road!"

"It ain't as if you won't see them again or scared, they got some cruel master what's gon' lash they backs or even make 'em slave in the hot sun," another reassured her. "I sure Mr. Danzee gon' teach them a trade and work 'em light. I don't know no White man 'round here seem mo' devoted to his colored chirren dan dat man. Lord, sometime he ack like he could kiss de groun' dey walk on."

Elizabeth wasn't even listening to the consolations of those who counseled acceptance of this fate. The only person she listened to was Reverend Brown, the free Negro jackleg minister who preached to slaves and free coloreds wherever he could gather them, read whatever they needed to have read, wrote whatever letters they had to write, circulated messages about slave meetings, passed the news for slave escapes and provided information of safe houses for runaways on the trek North.

Before the White folks, he was a humble and "good" nigger, even whispering some no-longer relevant information about underground activity—just enough to maintain his reputation among slaveowners as trustworthy. The slave and free Negro communities all protected him with a vengeance, and woe be unto the nigger that let slip anything that might jeopardize their leader. Elizabeth finally unsealed her eyes, ears, and mind when Reverend Brown started telling her about the process of appeal (in this case on the basis that her children were bound without her knowledge and consent). He informed her where to go at the Courthouse and when, but he warned her... her chances were meager, "not much more chance dan a snowball in hell," was what he said. Legally she could appeal, but the justices were all friends of Mr. Danzee's, and they weren't likely to rule against him and in favor of a colored woman, especially an unmarried one. She could get a lawyer, but you couldn't trust those White lawyers—they would charge her a great deal of money, maybe even take her house, and still not really do anything to help her win.

"When de judge is a fox, and de jury is foxes, and de

lawyers is foxes, ain't gon' be much justice for poor Sis Goose," Reverend Brown reminded her of the familiar tale of the goose who tried to assert her rights to sail on the lake free of molestation.

"Justice! *Justice!*" sneered Uncle Hesekiah. When White folks talk about justice, they mean 'just us.'"

"Yes, my child," Reverend Brown pitifully assented, "Getting even the few legal rights we have is mighty difficult in these folks' courts." He also warned her that on court days, she would be at the mercy of the crowd of drunken White men who gathered, cursing, quarreling, fighting, and riding their horses over the stiles and even the old tavern porch.

But there was the possibility of appeal, and Elizabeth was already planning her trip to the Courthouse the next day to find out what she could do to get her children back. Didn't matter if she had to sell her house and land. What good was house and land without her boys? She couldn't just...

But James was walking in the door, puzzled at all these people gathered around his wife.

It was a good thing so many friends and neighbors were there when James came home. When he saw his wife's shredded dress and the blood now dried on her back and learned what all had transpired while he was at the river, he was ready to go shoot the churchwardens what flayed her and took her boys *and* go kill somebody at Danzee's house as well.

"I might as well die like a *man!*" he screamed. "A man can't let them White sonsabitches come to they house and beat they wife and take they chirren!"

But the other men took and hid his gun and held him back, finally convincing him that he wouldn't help matters by getting himself (and maybe Elizabeth) killed. They had to remember little Will too. He still needed his mother and James. James's brother Josh and his uncle Samuel stayed at the house that night to be sure he didn't do anything rash, even if they had to physically restrain him.

James finally relented but vowed to himself that at least one of those White sonsabitches would pay ... but he'd be smart about it. The neighbors were right. No need to get hisself killed. What good would that do Elizabeth and her children?

James began to console himself with detailed planning of the ways he could exact some revenge. Hunting accidents were always happening in Charles City. Danzee loved to fish. There were things that could be done to boats, things that could be done in boats... Danzee had a new mulatto woman. A lot o' things could be done to a man when he had his pants down. Yes, he could wait, but he wouldn't forget. Some White man was gon' pay... someday...

Elizabeth came back from the Courthouse the next day, a beaten woman. She'd always felt a sense of empowerment because her mother was a White Englishwoman and her father a free colored man. That sense of privilege had been enhanced when Elizabeth became the pampered mistress of William Joseph Danzee, one of the biggest plantation owners in the county. She'd trembled on many occasions when she saw slaves lashed, she'd cried with distraught mothers and consoled friends whose family members were torn away, but she never doubted that she was immune from such a travesty—until they took her boys.

At the Courthouse, they treated her like a dog, made it clear that she'd be wasting her time to appeal, warned her that if she made Mr. Danzee mad, he might let John and Abraham be bound out to somebody else she didn't even know. He could let them be bound out to somebody *way*, way away, somebody dishonest who might just slave them until they were grown men and then *sell* 'em into slavery. They reminded her the boys were bound only until they were twenty-one, but if she wanted to raise a fuss about it, they could bind them until they were *thirty-one*.[1] They reminded her that they hadn't taken her third son, but the county needed to do something about "you wenches and all yo' illegitimate children." If she wanted to pester busy White men here at the Courthouse, maybe they could raise that issue for her.

"What is that other pickaninny's name?" one demanded, grabbing a pen and paper and mumbling about nigger wenches that didn't even appreciate how generous White folks were with them. The two justices who talked to her suggested that she was personally attacking them by questioning their judgment. Then they pointed to the whipping post with its uneven platform and the nails for the ears as a better place to deal with wenches guilty of whoredom

---

1 In 1765 a law limited service of "bastard children of women servants and Negroes or free Christian, white women by Negroes" to age twenty-one (Jane Purcell Guild, Black Laws of Virginia, 270).

and fornication. "A few public whippings and we wouldn't have all this shameful and abominable mixture of races and all these mixed bastards taking up time in our courts!" one forcefully concluded.

She fled home, feeling the weight of her blackness in a way she never had before. And, with the pain and hopelessness and helplessness that she now experienced as a colored woman, she also began for the first time to hate White people—she who had adored her White mother and who had been practically married to a White man for nine years—now knew that she *hated* all White people, including them—*especially* them.

And the very venom of her newly acquired hatred offered her some relief.

"I hate those red-faced bastards, *every* one of them," she hissed, uttering her first profanity ever and finding some release in repeating it: "Dirty bastards, filthy bastards, stinking bastards... low-down bastards... bastards ... *bastards!*"

CHAPTER TWO

A WHITE MOTHER
AND A WHITE LOVER

*The very time I thought I was lost, my
dungeon shook, and my chains fell off.*
- African American Proverb

Elizabeth had always felt certain she remembered
her mother's beauty; she was sure she remembered
how eloquently she read to her; she was sure she
remembered her beautiful British accent, which she still
tried to cultivate herself; she was sure she remembered
her mother's loving attention to her. But now one fact and
one fact only overshadowed all the years of mythmaking—
her mother had deserted her when she was just five years
old and had never contacted her again. Moll had gone back
to a comfortable life in England with her White lover and
had left her daughter to endure all the trials that await, not
merely an orphan, but a colored and female orphan in a
slave society. What kind of mother could do that?

What Elizabeth now knew she remembered—all she could
possibly remember—was a myth based on the framed picture of a gorgeous White woman dressed like British roy-
alty. For the first time, she was struck with the irony that

there was no image of the Black father who took care of her and protected her and told her all the lies about how beautiful and loving Moll was.... What kind of a name was Moll, anyway? The Elizabeth before that visit to the Courthouse would have actually been able to recall for us the warmth she felt cuddled in her mother's arms as she read to her on those evenings when Moll could get away from the plantation. Had Elizabeth told us about Moll before her trip to the Courthouse, her portrait would have been mawkishly romantic; after the trip to the Courthouse, any portrait she painted would be as black as the ashes of that picture she threw in the fireplace as soon as she stormed back in her house.

What Elizabeth did not know—could not know—was that Moll had had a hard life too.

Moll's own mother, convicted of a felony for petty theft, had saved herself from The Old Bailey by agreeing to be transported to a plantation in the colonies no more than two years after she gave birth to the child in 1698. Moll was raised by Dame Lydia Austin, a poor, but educated woman with whom the magistrates of Colchester placed her. The woman fed the orphan and taught her to read and write and to work with a needle.

By the time she was fifteen, Moll's linens and laces and dresses became so much admired throughout the neighborhood that she found herself frequently in the homes of the well-to-do, designing, and mending for them. Moll had such a beautiful face, such a pleasing figure, such exquisite clothes, such a lively personality, that varied gentlewomen of the town took her for months to live in their houses or to accompany them on vacations as a companion for their daughters. In such circumstances, she learned from the masters employed to teach the young ladies of the house right along with her superiors, often excelling them in her mastery of music and dance and French and composition. This exposure, her ready intelligence, and her determination to be a gentlewoman like those in whose homes she now spent most of her time, soon molded her into an exquisite model of the finest of British gentlewomen of the period—except, of course, for the matter of blood.

Thus it was that Moll met the daughters of Viscount Robert Stanford, one of the Ministers of King George I, when they were visiting friends with whom Moll was vacationing as a companion. The Stanford girls fell in love with the smart, vivacious Moll and begged her to come to their London residence and design some clothes for them for their upcoming trip to Paris. Moll, not unconscious of what a move up in society this would be, readily assented, and on October 4, 1715, all the neighbors in her Colchester community were aghast to see the minister's coach pull in front of the home of Dame Austin to pick up Moll. She strutted out of the house like a lady accustomed to such service, directed where her bags were to be collected, took the arm of the coachman, and stepped into the carriage.

Here as elsewhere, Moll found herself quickly feeling more and more comfortable with the elegance of her surroundings. Here as elsewhere, though she provided the services of a seamstress and a lady's maid, she became a popular companion, invited to go for a horseback ride, to form a part of a musical ensemble, to perform with the young ladies of the household in a play, to help them with their French and composition, even to join them in their bedrooms for girls' talk.

Precisely four days after Moll's entrance into London, Viscount Robert Stanford laid eyes on her for the first time as she chatted animatedly with his daughters having tea on the south portico of his Westminster home. He could never thereafter take his eyes off her. He subtly inquired about their visitor and was delighted to learn she was the poor bastard child of a deported felon, despite the fact she looked more royal than his daughters and spoke as eloquently as any British lady. Her condition gave him cause to hope he might have some opportunity to realize the desire that groped him the moment he laid eyes on her for the first time.

Viscount Stanford, though old enough to be Moll's father, was yet a dashing specimen of a man, well experienced in appealing to the sentiments of a vulnerable young woman. He wasted no time in finding an opportunity to be alone with his beautiful guest. He quickly fell to his knees, confessed he had fallen in love with Moll, begged her to allow him to arrange a rendezvous, where they could talk at some length, promising her that everything would be handled in such a way as not to compromise her good name, and assuring her his motives were honest and aboveboard. He was, he confessed with teary eyes and trembling lips, miserable in his marriage, and as soon as he could settle matters in his family, he was going to get a divorce. He hoped Moll would meet with him so they could discuss a possible future together. He could not imagine a more beautiful and accomplished person than herself to be the kind of wife that he required in his constant role in the palace, where a fat old lady like his present wife, who knew nothing more to talk about than her gout, was an embarrassment.

Moll was willingly, even eagerly, seduced. In a few days, she found herself alone in a comfortable inn with Viscount Stanford. No sooner had the door closed than he gathered her in his arms and planted a lingering kiss on her trembling lips. Moll sighed with pleasure, and, clasping her arms around his neck, she eagerly awaited another kiss... But he had already run his hand up her dress and begun to tug on her undergarments. Moll was indeed frightened at his urgency and begged him to stop. She knew she should keep her drawers up and her dress down as she had been taught to do by Dame Lydia. She knew women should never let men tumble them before marriage. She knew men tried to seduce any woman they could. She knew they never married women who succumbed—they wanted a virgin on their marriage night. How many times had Dame Lydia reminded her, "A man won't buy the cow when he can get the milk for free"? She knew that marriage to Stanford was certainly not presently a possibility. Moll knew all these things, and she was determined that talk about marriage should precede what Stanford was now trying to do. She resisted.

But the more she tried to prevent him from reaching his goal, the more excited he became. He eased her down on the bed and pressed his chest against her bosom, while he used one leg to pry her thighs apart, his hands excitedly but gently stroking and probing her hot, quivering, but taut maidenhead.

He moaned. Moll sighed.

All the lessons, all the warnings were forgotten as her mind closed down. She was one mass of tingly feelings she had never even imagined before—all emanating from those spots that Stanford was caressing. Nothing else mattered.

He moaned. She sighed.

Easing her legs still further apart, he pulled himself astride her body and attempted to force entry into her unyielding vagina. Moll groaned, frightened by the sudden pain.

The resistance of her hymen gave him pause. He did not want this experience to be frightening or painful for Moll. Restraining the powerful desire to possess this treasure, to immediately taste this virgin delight, he bit his lips and summoned up difficult self-control. Ceasing his efforts to penetrate, he calmed and soothed his delicious prize, whispering sweet nothings in her ear. When finally he entered her, the slight pain that elicited a scream was nothing to the delight that her quivering body felt as they started riding this wave whose crest they both sought. Nothing ... nothing—not even sure death—could have made either pause or turn back now. Moll, as aroused as Stanford, returned his thrusts so boldly, caressed his head, his neck, his back, so passionately, whispered in his ear so wantonly that, were it not for the bloody sheets, the Viscount might have doubted that she was indeed an inexperienced virgin.

The Viscount, finding himself more smitten with Moll than he had envisaged, decided to settle her in a well-positioned apartment convenient to his home and his work. Indeed, before long, he actually appeared publicly with her, much to the humiliation of his family. That he might have a mistress was an annoying reality, such as countless families in and around the court accepted and lived with.

That so prominent a minister as Viscount Stanford would flaunt her before the very daughters who had brought the viper into their home as their own friend was more than the mother and daughters could bear.

Viscount Stanford had recently managed to vex His Royal Highness as well. King George I, who had expelled a Tory minister to appoint Viscount Stanford one of his ministers, was greatly perplexed that so trusted a member of his court as Stanford had recently publicly criticized His Royal Highness for his treatment of his wife, Sophia Dorothea of Celle, whom he had held imprisoned since 1694 for her infidelity. Besides, Stanford had leveled vicious charges against both of the King's beloved mistresses. Not only did Stanford seem to be conniving with Sophia to humiliate him, but he was even now joining forces with the King's treacherous son, George Augustus, Prince of Wales. King George was fuming about this behavior when he was visited by a trusted messenger sent by Viscountess Lenora Stanford.

The timing was perfect.

A plot was about to be formed by the two most powerful foes of Viscount Stanford—foes who a few months ago had been his closest allies. In a matter of three days, before the victims knew what was happening to them, trumped-up charges of the theft of valuable jewels from the Stanford girls had landed Moll aboard one of His Majesty's ships to the Virginia Colony to serve seven years of indenture to William Joseph Danzee. All of this took place suddenly, with Stanford conveniently dispatched to France on state business. It was to be more than four years before one of Moll's letters finally reached him, and he learned where she was and exactly what kind of plot had torn her away from him.

Meanwhile, Moll, who had for a few months enjoyed a truly royal life in England, now experienced the rough crossing of the Atlantic and the even rougher life of an indentured servant on a Virginia Plantation.

Placed at first in the fields to work alongside the slaves, Moll might have perished had it not been for the strong arms of Abraham, a free Negro who worked for wages during the busy summer months on Yorkshire Plantation. Abraham easily did his work and half of hers and then fixed her a nourishing meal in his nearby cabin so she wouldn't have to subsist on the gruel allotted to the indentures. Every evening, when Moll rode off on Abraham's steed, seated sidesaddle in front of him, she felt as if he were her hero, whisking her away from the hell into which she had been cast. When later Mrs. Danzee discovered Moll's talents with the needle and moved her into the house for lighter tasks, Moll was already accustomed to spending the night with Abraham, and despite the disapproval of all around her, she quietly slipped away most evenings to meet him in the woods by the creek and gallop off to his cabin.

Moll was not restrained in her relations by the usual prejudices against Negroes. She had never had any acquaintance with any colored people before she was indentured, and since then, she had found them to be far nicer to her than any of the Whites with whom she had dealings. Indeed, she was mesmerized by the striking physique of the six-foot-two-inch Abraham, whose tan complexion was a blending of his African mother's dark skin and her Indian husband's lighter complexion. The heaviest, blackest, straightest hair she had ever seen hung about his tall, broad shoulders. Proper White women, unable to avoid staring at this gorgeous specimen of manhood, blushed as they tried to avert their gaze. Thus, though Moll missed the glamour and elegance of the courtly life and the attentions of her aged, White paramour, she was never more content than she felt in the arms of her young, sable lover.

The reader may wonder if Moll considered marriage to Abraham. As an indentured servant, marriage was out of the question without her master's express permission, but Act XVI of the State of Virginia, passed in 1691, made that impossible in her case: "whatsoever English or other white man or woman, bond or free, shall intermarry with a Negro, mulatto, or Indian man or woman, bond or free, he shall within three months be banished from this dominion forever."

So Moll and Abraham jumped the broom.

By the time their daughter, Elizabeth, was born in 1717, Moll's life in England seemed like a distant dream. The child was beautiful, and Moll felt an occasional brief pang of guilt that she experienced no maternal compassion. She was happy to turn over most of the childrearing to Abraham's mother, whom she, like Abraham, called Nana. A former slave who had been purchased by her Indian lover, Nana, now long a widow, moved in with Abraham and spent her days pampering her only grand. The baby gave new meaning to a life that she had found empty and meaningless since her husband died more than ten years ago. Some nights Moll pretended she couldn't get away from the plantation so she wouldn't have to be awakened by the crying baby and so that she wouldn't be required to change and wash dirty diapers. On such occasions, the services of a wet nurse were secured by the proud father. In emergencies, the baby was provided with a rag tiddy. The baby was weaned early, and Moll found more and more excuses to spend more time on the plantation.

Before she knew it, the child was toddling and then talking. She dutifully called Moll Mother, but always looked at her as if to say, "Who is this stranger?"

Moll, torn by guilt, started reading to the child in the evenings when she came home. When she read, the child relaxed, even curled up in this stranger's lap. As Elizabeth listened to the beautiful British cadences, she decided that this stranger was some lovely and magical White goddess. This rare image of Moll, beautiful hands holding a magical book, melodic voice spinning enthralling tales as she cuddled the child in her arms, became the vision that Elizabeth held on to all of her life ... that is, until that fateful trip to the Courthouse. She had treasured and stored this memory, though Moll had returned to England before Elizabeth realized the beautiful stranger/mother had not visited in such a long time that she was never going to come again.

When the English messenger appeared at William Joseph Danzee's door on December 1, 1722, with papers signed by Viscount Stanford and a draft to reimburse Danzee for the time remaining on Moll's indenture, Moll did not waste much time in unproductive worry about those who had become her family since she left the Viscount. All she could think about was a return to her luxurious apartment and her comfortable life in England. If a thought that there were a husband and a child to consider ever entered her mind, she brushed it aside as a foolish consideration. Moll reflected in a way she never had before on just how harshly she was regarded in Virginia because of her relationship with the Negroes. She knew that legally she could have her period of indenture extended because she had had a bastard child by a Negro man, she could be fined, and even jailed, and her child could be indentured. Thus, she rationalized, by leaving, she would not only remove herself from the risk of punishment under the miscegenation law of Virginia, but she would also protect her child from indenture.

Recognizing that she would not be restored to her former life as a favored mistress of Viscount Stanford with a mixed child, she never entertained any thought of taking Elizabeth with her. Rather she hastened to Abraham's when she knew he would not be home and begged Nana to explain to her daughter and Abraham that she could not pass up this opportunity to return to England. She did not even bother to go in to kiss the sleeping child goodbye, fearful, she claimed, that it might wake her. A few tears fell as she begged Nana to tell Abraham and Elizabeth how painful it was for her to leave them here. She placed in Nana's hands her portrait, painted before she left England, begging her to tell Abraham and Elizabeth that she left this picture as a symbol, signifying her continuing spirit with her family in the colonies. She did not say she would write to them. She did not speak of any possibility of ever seeing them in the future.

When Elizabeth realized Moll was no longer coming to visit them, she pulled out her books and read the stories herself, recognizing some words, but remembering the plots well enough to convince anyone who didn't know better that she was actually reading. She read in a British accent that even then, with the encouragement of her father and grandmother, she began to cultivate. Proud of his daughter's achievements, Abraham took her to the home of Reverend Brown, a literate free Negro who continued the lessons Moll had begun, so that by the time Elizabeth was eight, she could read the Bible to her proud father and grandmother. She also seemed to have inherited Moll's talent with the needle, and with just the minutest lessons from her Nana, she was soon creating beautiful handiwork.

Mistress Jane Danzee was delighted to discover Elizabeth's talents. She had not enjoyed any elegant needlework since Moll had returned to England twelve years ago. Once Elizabeth had done a few jobs for her, Mistress Danzee couldn't get enough of the talented seamstress. She had her brought to Yorkshire Plantation to embroider table linens, to design and sew dresses, to repair the lace on her fine gowns, to knit socks and hats for gifts; she seemed to look for jobs to hire the blossoming teenage mulatto.

Elizabeth, having inherited her mother's taste for elegance, enjoyed the time she spent at the beautiful plantation house, sewing, for the most part, in the sunny workroom, but occasionally browsing through the leather-bound books in the adjoining library ... which was where she was when she was discovered one day by William Joseph Danzee. Frightened that she would be reprimanded for trespassing in Mr. Danzee's private study, she turned to him with pleading eyes and blushing cheeks; but before she could utter any explanation, he smiled at her, rebuked any efforts at an apology, and asked, "So ... you like to read, do you?"

Elizabeth did not deny her literacy as most colored girls would have done; rather, returning his smile, she confessed her love of literature and added that she had had so little opportunity to enjoy reading because she had so few books. She did not apologize, as most colored girls would have done, but added, "I have never seen so many interesting books as you have here. It must take you a lifetime to read them."

"Well, perhaps then you will help me get through this

library. There are a couple of interesting novels that I think you would enjoy," he laughed, pulling two down from the shelf and deliberately touching her delicate hands as he placed the books there. Elizabeth trembled nervously but feared to withdraw her hands lest the books be removed. If the truth be told, she was so excited by the obvious flirtation of this handsome, slightly graying squire, who spoke and dressed like no one she had ever met before, that she had no real desire to escape his company or even his flirtations.

Alas, Elizabeth had no mother to warn her of the outcome of these advances from handsome, mature gentry. Elizabeth, poor dear, was even more vulnerable than Moll had been, burdened as she was with olive skin in a racist society. Elizabeth no longer even had the loving care of her father and her grandmother, both of whom had left her for a land even more distant than that to which Moll had fled. Indeed, Elizabeth was reminded of her father's protectiveness in the generosity and gentleness of this graying Cavalier, who was now whispering in her ear that he would visit her soon and bring her a special book that he wanted to buy for her when he next went to Richmond.

Elizabeth, too excited to sew one straight stitch for the rest of the evening, returned to her lonely home with two dresses she hadn't yet hemmed for Mrs. Danzee. Musing happily about the upcoming visit from Mr. Danzee, she did not allow herself to recall the many warnings her recently departed father had issued about protecting herself from White men. Indeed, Fa seemed always to be warning her about men. She had to be careful about the Negro boys, who were always seeking to talk to her and bringing her gifts of flowers and fresh fish and watermelons from their gardens. Those boys had nothing to offer her. The

Indians were not much better, he painfully admitted. They had been beaten and scattered so much and were so taken with spirituous liquors that one could no longer find brave warriors like his own great-grandfather, a member of the powerful Chickahominy Tribe who had fought with Opechancanough (brother of Powhatan) when he made his last desperate effort to drive the English out of their land in 1644 and killed more than 500 settlers. And worst of all were White men, who never did anything but take advantage of Negro women and leave them to raise their bastard children alone. Even worse, some of them would take the children and put them to work with their slaves. No respectable Negro man would want her after she had been used by a White man.

There was a way out of this dilemma, Abraham insisted. As long as she could remember, he had told her that he wanted her to move to Canada as soon as she was eighteen. There was a little brown leather packet carefully hidden in a chest that he kept ready for that journey. In it was enough money for her to book passage on a ship and to get a room in a boarding house until she could establish her sewing business there. There was also the name of someone that Reverend Brown knew in Toronto who would help her. Abraham had it all worked out. Her free papers were kept there as well since he did not allow her to go any further than their little community, where even the White people knew her and would never threaten to kidnap her into slavery. A heavy coat and sweater and some other clothing that had been left by Moll were also in the bag, as well as a Bible. There was a little doll that he had carved for her when she was little... "something to remember your old Fa by."

"Oh, no, I'll never leave you, Fa," she protested.

But her Fa had left her, suddenly and unexpectedly just before her seventeenth birthday. And just as suddenly and unexpectedly, all the warnings he had preached to her flew out of her mind the moment she looked out of the door and saw William Joseph Danzee spring from his steed and tie him to the post in her back yard. It was so easy to forget her father's warnings as she felt protected for the first time since her Fa's death by the arms of a strong man around her, as she felt herself pampered by the special gifts with which he forever surprised her. William Joseph Danzee brought books and clothes and chocolates. Elizabeth felt like the beautiful damsels who were pursued by dashing young suitors in the novels she loved so passionately.

Danzee was fascinated by Elizabeth as well. Her olive complexion, her green eyes, her red curls presented an exotic combination that excited him. He painted her, he bought dresses to compliment her skin, her eyes, her hair. He visited her practically every day and spent some nights. He even took her once or twice to Williamsburg with him. He found her not only a refreshing and exotic sex partner, but he enjoyed talking with her. She knew more of the literary classics than his wife, and he delighted in her unexpected responses to some of the novels they read together. They sometimes had animated debates about everything from Shakespeare to the Bible—even slavery. They both agreed that slavery was evil and lamented the fact that economics forced his continued involvement in that hated system. She read the novels he gave her with such flair and drama that they occasionally spent a whole evening together with her reading and, at times enacting certain scenes for him. Never having been outside of Charles City until he took her to Williamsburg, she delighted in his accounts of the world outside—Richmond, Washington,

New York, London. She knew little of life but relished experiencing it, if only through books and his accounts. Her enthusiasm titillated him. He often dreamed of running off with her to one of these distant places and leaving his nagging and aging wife behind forever.

That, of course, was just a dream. His livelihood was in his plantation, and one had to be close to oversee the 130 slaves who worked the place. Then there was his daughter, for whom he had responsibility, though he delighted little in her company. Mary was too much like her mother—concerned only about petty gossip and clothes and ...; he couldn't think what else concerned her—she seemed so artificially limited, like her mother. Nothing elicited a truly exuberant response or any really heartfelt emotion. He had taught her to ride, and though she religiously mounted her horse at least twice a week and went through the motions, she seemed to feel no love for the sport or for the thoroughbred stallion he had bought for her. Her face bore the same tense and strained look whether she trotted or galloped, whether she cantered or cleared a fence. She never talked to the horse, she never yelled at him, she never reached down to caress his neck. She managed a little smile if her father applauded her style and seemed to work hard to win his approval, but she, herself, obviously found little personal delight in the sport. Here, as elsewhere, her range from joy and laughter through passion to anger seemed so limited.

Unlike Danzee's olive sons, who even at three and five ran so hard they fell down panting, laughed so hard the tears ran down their eyes, wrangled for his attention when he arrived so energetically the animals all bolted in fear. And yet these energetic fellows would sit patiently by his side on the riverbank waiting for a bite on their fish line.

He couldn't believe how heartbroken they could be if they caught no fish, how excited they were when something tugged on their line. This was life, and he was proud to be their father. He couldn't wait to take them hunting— they were already begging their mother to let them go with him, but she had insisted that they weren't old enough. He gave in to Elizabeth as he usually did, so happy was he to have this pastoral home to which he could escape from the headaches and boredom of Yorkshire Plantation.

Over the years, he added a parlor and a bedroom to Elizabeth's small cottage, overseeing its construction himself. He had a walnut Queen Anne bedroom suite and a living room sofa and table delivered from Richmond on the first Christmas after their second son, John, was born. Elizabeth's dresser featured the elaborately carved cabriole legs that were so popular throughout the colonies before the Revolution.

By the time their third son was born, Danzee was no less excited about his progeny, but he was less and less thrilled with Elizabeth's widening waist and her drooping breasts. She seemed to have no time for their erstwhile pastime of reading, and when she did, it was almost a monotone, none of the youthful dramatization entering her renditions. In recent years, she began to have as much to complain about as Mrs. Danzee. She was lonely. Her Negro neighbors feared to come to visit her lest they embarrass him by their presence. Her sons wanted to know why they couldn't call him daddy and why they couldn't talk about their father to their friends. She wanted to go to church and the quiltings and games that her neighbors enjoyed—and she couldn't understand why she always had to be home just waiting until he got a notion to stop by. She didn't tell him that she wanted to get married, she wanted a husband who could take her out, she wanted a husband who could dance, she wanted a husband who could sing with her the church songs she loved and some of the other Negro ditties she could never ever let him know she knew. She wanted a husband she didn't have to call "Mister." She wanted a husband who lived with her. She wanted a husband to grow old with. She couldn't tell him these last things, but they worked on her mind and found expression in an attitude that silently conveyed more than she intended about her dissatisfaction with their relationship.

Danzee's visits became less and less frequent, shorter, and shorter. It was clear that he came now mainly to see his sons. He rarely ate a meal. He never stayed all night. He never took her anywhere.

The crisis arose when he came one Saturday and found her and Martha Seldorn cleaning chitterlings while James Seldorn, the free Negro who lived up near Wilcox Wharf, was just removing a slab of pork ribs from some hot coals. Danzee had tied his horse out front and walked around the back before either James or Elizabeth heard him. What he had heard was voices raised in song and then collapsing in loud and gleeful laughter such as he had forgotten his paramour was capable of. Both James and Elizabeth abruptly terminated their laughter mid-point, but they could not erase the sparkle in their eyes.

"Good afternoon, Mr. Danzee," James broke the silence. "You just in time for a taste of Old Bertha. My sister Martha and me come help our neighbor with the butchering."

After a long silence, James continued, this time addressing Elizabeth, "We'll be on our way now. We'll come back tomorrow to help you smoke your hams and make some souse."

"I'm gon' take a couple o' these ribs with me for dinner, Elizabeth... if you can spare 'em," Martha chimed in, both avoiding any recognition of Danzee's sullen demeanor, and smiling as they politely bade him goodbye.

The final ignominy, Danzee thought at the time, was James' whispered assurance to Elizabeth that he would linger nearby in case she needed him. Danzee, whose furor had ignited James's concern for Elizabeth's safety, had not heard what he whispered to her, but the brazen nerve of that nigger whispering in his woman's ear with him standing right there infuriated him to the point where he would have tied her up and whipped her right then and there if his sons had not been there clamoring for his attention and wondering why he was ignoring them. The final ignominy, he later understood, was that when she turned to him as they left, she still retained the glow that had excited him when he caught her reading in his library and fell in love with her. He felt his nature rising and wanted to take her right then and there, smelling as she did of pig's intestines. But he couldn't lower himself to sharing a woman with a nigger, and even if she hadn't been intimate with James—and he was sure she hadn't—he knew he had lost her...

"You and the boys won't ever want for anything," he assured her later, after her friends had left. "I'll see to that." He paused before he turned to leave, allowing time for her to beg him not to desert her. The painful final ignominy, he would always remember, was the relief he saw in her eyes that he was bidding her adieu.

"Thank you. You're a good man, Mr. Danzee," she replied, more in pity for him than in thanks for his generosity and certainly not in apology for allowing herself to be caught in a situation that declared her return to the Negro community. He knew too that when she said, "You're a good man," she meant good for a White man.

He rushed to the front yard and his horse to avert his desire to claim her body one last time and be hurt even more to be rejected for a nigger. He thought seriously about at least hitting her one time with his whip, but instead, he finally responded to his nonplussed sons: "Meet me at the creek in the morning at seven, and we'll fish and roast our catch on the shore, whatdoyousay?"

He left the boys jumping up and down, cheering, and Elizabeth as happy as they.

"Why in the hell am I so sad when everybody else is in such a good mood?" he asked himself, as he rode away, passing James standing at the creek, putting on a show of fishing, his back to the road as if unaware of Danzee's movements.

Danzee solemnly swore to himself that the nigger bitch would pay for humiliating him after all he had done for her.

CHAPTER THREE

JAMES SELDORN'S REVENGE

The strong men... coming on
The strong men gittin' stronger
Strong men...
Stronger...
                    - Sterling A. Brown, "Strong Men"

James Seldorn was born in a land where men were either free or slave, and he was neither. If a so-called free colored man could no nothing to prevent his free wife's children from being taken away from her and apprenticed to their White father, he certainly wasn't any better off than a slave. For the year since Abraham and John had been bound to Danzee, James had felt himself less and less of a man. There was an emptiness and a silence in the home he shared with Elizabeth that constantly reminded him that he could protect neither his children or his wife. No matter how hard he tried, he could do nothing to console her. She had lost all interest in life, in work, in sewing, in cooking, in eating, even in participating in the community activities that had begun to bring her such joy after James had moved in with her.

Remembering those months of pleasure was what made the present so painful. Instead of sitting up in the balcony of a White church, Elizabeth had started joining James and his Negro friends (slave and free) in their services led by Reverend Brown in a little log cabin hidden in the woods. She had felt herself come alive with the ecstasy of the singing and dancing of the worshippers. They clapped their hands, swayed their bodies, tossed their heads, and exuberantly praised the Lord as they shuffled around in a ring shout. At first, she had sat still, enjoying the spirit of the meeting without entering into it fully, but lately, she had been rising and singing praises to the Lord as if she had been shouting all her life. They had even gone to a few outdoor revivals and camp meetings outside of Charles City—in James City and New Kent. They had never heard the term, but they were among those who lived the Great Awakening.

Elizabeth had, for the first time, gone to cornshuckings, quilting bees, even a fish fry down on the James River.

And *dances*! James had talked her into going to one of the dances where the slaves and some free Blacks mingled almost every Saturday night. There was always a "band," most of them slaves from the nearby plantations. Old Nicodemus was always there playing that fiddle his master bought him—and Dick was picking his old banjo. Sometimes there was a drummer beating sticks on an old washtub, or somebody blowing on quills made out of reeds, or somebody shaking his homemade tambourines.

Elizabeth had sat back and laughed and clapped and cheered the couples in the middle of the floor, dancing a wild jig. Feet flying, hips twitching, each couple seemed to be trying to outdo the others. Some displayed more fancy and intricate leg work, feet tapping or executing subtle maneuvers; some swung, twisted, or gyrated their hips; still others executed marvelous and complicated shoulder and arm and head movements. A few beat their hands on their thighs and legs or even their heels and heads. They all moved in a mesmerizing rhythm, sliding, spinning, finding new and challenging movements to execute with every part of their bodies. After everybody danced out, they sat down to a big feast. Then they had the big competitions. Two or three of the women would shuffle out on the floor with a glass of water on their heads and see who could do the most intricate steps without spilling the water. Then the men would compete, patting Juba, taking the floor one at a time. After one had slapped Juba till his hands were tingling and performed his specialties, cutting the pigeon wing and what have you, then the second man would ease on out on the floor and do his thing:

Juba dis,
Juba dat
Juba kill a yaller cat.

The band played, and the people sang, and those dancers carried on. Oh, I tell you, there were some good times at those Saturday night frolics!

But the first time Elizabeth went to one of the dances with James, she was so awed by so much talent, she had begged off when James asked her to go on the floor. Then she had to try to hide her jealousy when James stepped out on the floor with that single mulatto gal, Polly, her laughing and shaking her hips while everybody shouted for more, more, more. "Dance ole Jenny down," they screamed, using a popular acclamation, not referring to anyone in particular. They would even pass the word about a forthcoming dance by saying to someone, "We gon' dance ole Jenny down tonight."

Elizabeth sat mortified. She silently vowed that next

time her man was not gon' be dancing ole Jenny down with no Polly... or no other wench. So she took notes of the dance steps and went home and practiced when nobody was around. She soon discovered that some of the movements she remembered from the children's games she used to play offered some basic steps for the dances. The rhythms of the ring shouts—with a freeing of the feet—likewise could be transposed to the dance floor. Elizabeth hummed and danced while she worked all the next week, sometimes pausing to practice a hip swivel or a little jig. She laughed out loud at herself—a self she hardly recognized, but a self she liked so much she gave herself a big hug.

The next Saturday night, Elizabeth dressed up in a fancy dress she had worked on all week. She penned her hair up in a popular style like the White women wore. Tonight, she was gon' be the queen of the ball.

As soon as they arrived and had spoken to a few friends, she announced, "James, if you don't mind teaching me, I want to dance."

Though Elizabeth was not yet a Polly on the floor, her friends all crowded around and encouraged her, happy that she had stopped acting so stiff and proud and had loosened up enough to shake her hips. "Dance ole Jenny down," they shouted! James whirled her around, slowly at first, and then faster and faster. Then they joined a line dance. Elizabeth laughed and danced, joked with the womenfolk and danced, drank homemade wine, and danced. She was having such a good time that she was no longer disturbed when in some of the ring dances, she and James moved around to other partners. Elizabeth danced almost all night, and her feet were still dancing when she and James dragged in their front door and collapsed on the bed, the sound of the banjo still ringing in her head.

The new Elizabeth, relaxed and free, dancing and singing, found expression in the couple's loving too. As one who had smiled contentedly as if she were a third party as she had witnessed Mr. Danzee in the throes of passion, Elizabeth was surprised to find herself moaning and groaning, grinding and thrusting, moving with her lover to that height where they both exploded, and he had to stifle her yells to keep her from waking her children. Life for Elizabeth and James was beautiful and exciting. Even the children reveled in this new life, entering enthusiastically into their new church worship and enjoying this unfamiliar mother whose lips smiled and whose eyes twinkled. They liked having a full-time father in the house. They liked calling someone "Pa." They missed Mr. Danzee's visits and his gifts and their fishing trips, but they had found themselves uncomfortable the few times he had sent for them. He always asked so many questions about their mother and James, and, as young and inexperienced in the ways of adults as they were, they intuitively knew to provide as little information as possible to Mr. Danzee and to say nothing about these inquisitions to James and Elizabeth. They, too, were beginning to enjoy entering into the life of the Negro community—and to feel the threat of the White world.

James, unaware of this burden on the boys, had known nothing but complete happiness with his new wife and his new family.

But now, with Elizabeth's boys snatched from her, everything had changed. If James asked her to, she followed along to a church service or a visit with friends, or even a dance, but her heart was no longer in it. She sat as if in a daze, never singing, never responding to anyone without their having to call her name and repeat what they said. At a dance, she didn't seem to hear the music, and if she got up on the floor, she moved like a zombie.

The only time she displayed any interest or energy was when she attempted to sneak a message or some covered dish to her boys, or when they sent a note to her. She would sit and read and reread the note, then hold it and silently cry. James's attempts to console her were futile. He felt like some invisible man she hardly saw or heard, though she faithfully and pitifully tried to acknowledge his efforts.

And Will—Will missed his older brothers, but he missed his mother even more. She cared for him like an automaton. She sometimes forgot to fix his meals, to call him in from play in the evenings, even to guide him through his lessons. Occasionally he would read his lesson to her and realize that she had not heard a word he said; she sat mute when he asked what a word was. If it hadn't been for Pa Seldorn, he would never have had anyone to talk to or play with. Will was ashamed to admit that he sometimes wished he were at Mr. Danzee's with Abraham and John.

As for Elizabeth, she would certainly have simply walked out in the James River and never come back if it weren't for Will. She spent most of her time plotting ways to communicate with her older sons and to protect Will from a similar fate. She kept her eyes and ears on the alert for the return of the churchwardens who had come with that first court order to take her two older boys away, and she devised a million responses if they attempted to take her last son. She rehearsed the scenarios over and over in her mind. Sometimes she raised her rifle and calmly shot the men as they rode up in her yard. In other cases, she chopped them down with an ax or a machete or a butcher knife when they attempted to hand her the court order. In some scenarios, she grabbed Will and ran out the back door, hiding in the woods. In this latter plot, the two of them made their way to Canada, evading bloodhounds and paterollers until they reached safety. So intense were these dramas in her mind that Elizabeth would find her heart pounding, her breath panting, and her brow sweating. She had no shortage of means devised, planned, dramatized, replayed—means to prevent the capture of her last son.

The day she had dreaded came almost exactly one year after the churchwardens first rode into her yard. When she saw them coming this second time, she could not remember even one of the means of escape she had so conscientiously devised. Frozen in her tracks, she stood, a mute bystander watching as tears silently rolled down her cheeks. Passively she received the court order they handed to her, never ever glancing at it and certainly not attempting to read it. She blankly looked at them when they asked if she wanted to gather some clothes for Will, until, finally, impatient with this foolish mute woman, they ordered him to gather up his things himself. She never even thought to tell them that she and James were now properly married. She could not lift a hand to resist nor utter a word of protest as they took her last son and rode off with him to serve William Joseph Danzee until he attained the age of twenty-one. She couldn't remember later whether she even said goodbye.

When James Seldorn returned home a couple of hours later that evening, she was still standing, a wobbly wraith, in the yard. If anyone had even lightly touched her on her shoulder, her trembling legs would have given way. Having cried until there were no more tears, she sobbed loud gasps as if she could not catch her breath. James needed no explanation. He picked her up and took her into the house. There were no words to be said—they had all been rehearsed to no avail before. He fixed her some tea, which sat there and turned cold as she lifted it a few times to her mouth when he pleaded with her to take a sip, but each time after a few minutes, she set it back down as if the task of swallowing were more than she could attempt.

The neighbors, hearing the news, descended upon the house again with their efforts at consolation, their expressions of anger, their advice, their prayers, their food offerings. This time she paid no attention to anything that was said by anyone. There was no hope, she knew that. William Joseph Danzee had exacted the ultimate punishment because he found her laughing with a Black man.

Late that night James Seldorn left his wife lying in their bed staring at the ceiling, and went out into his toolshed, gathered up some utensils, saddled his horse, and set out to enact one of the scenarios of revenge he had plotted for a year. In some of the scenes he envisioned, he walked up to William Joseph Danzee, looked him in the face, told him that he had to die for what he had done to Elizabeth, and proceeded either to shoot him in the head, throw him off a cliff or slowly and viciously beat him to death. In his mind, James concocted a plethora of diabolical plots to destroy Danzee. In some of the scenarios, he sneaked to his plantation house and set it on fire, or he slipped some poison in his food. In other schemes, he cut through the wheel bolts on Danzee's carriage just enough so that the wheels would come loose whenever the horses sped up; or he drilled a small hole in his boat so that it would slowly take on water and sink when he was out in the river; or he rigged some heavy steel object over the doorway, contrived to fall on him as he walked in his stables; or he set some trap that would snatch him up in a tree when he stepped on it, leaving him hanging upside down by his ensnared leg until he died; or he dug some big hole and covered it with dirt and branches so that he would fall in and the dirt would cover and suffocate him. James's devious plots became more and more implausible, but now he was about to stop fantasizing and execute the one design that he knew was the perfect one. He didn't reflect, as he had in his earlier carefully devised plots, on how he could possibly do this without getting caught. Consequence was immaterial. The sole reason his present design presented itself to him as the ideal vengeance was that it would make Danzee know something of a parent's grief upon the loss of a child. Danzee must suffer the same pain he had caused Elizabeth.

James Seldorn rode up to the carefully laid out tracks where Mary Danzee mechanically put her horse through his paces twice weekly. He went to the seventh obstacle over which she jumped. He took out the necessary tools and equipment from his bag and carefully raised that obstacle... just enough... He probably recognized that this scheme didn't have to work, that somebody else might get hurt, that a million things could go wrong, but he was certain that Mary would go out for a ride this Saturday morning the way she always did and that he had raised the obstacle just enough to cause a nasty fall for her and her horse.

When Elizabeth heard the news that William Joseph Danzee's daughter had been fatally injured when her horse's hooves tore down rather than jumped over an obstacle, throwing her to the ground so hard that it broke her neck, she wondered if it had anything to do with James Seldorn's venture out last night. But she refused to allow herself to seriously entertain that possibility. She was surprised that she almost felt a moment's sympathy for the father who had been riding behind his fated daughter.

Danzee's last thought before the accident was amazement at how beautifully Mary was riding that morning. She had raised forward from the saddle as she started her jump, and he had swelled with pride at her form. But then, suddenly, inexplicably, the horse seemed caught in midair, wrestling with the obstacle, while his daughter continued forward. Danzee heard a thud as she hit the ground, head-first. He quickly dismounted and rushed to his daughter's side. She lay on the ground, her body facing one way and her head the other. He knew better than to try to force her head back around to where it belonged, but he hoped he could relieve her pitiable gasping for air as her body twitched madly like a beheaded chicken in its final death throes. Having to do something in a situation that was obviously hopeless, the hapless father knelt down and desperately tried to force breath into his daughter's mouth. By the time Dr. Byrd had rushed to the scene, Mary was already dead, and her distraught father was still attempting to blow air through her cold lips. Everybody said it was amazing how little indication of injury there was— she looked beautiful lying there, no cuts, no scratches, no blood, just her head turned the wrong way, looking behind her. It was a vision the hapless father would carry with him to his grave.

William Joseph Danzee knew the pain of the loss of a child.

But James Seldorn did not experience the relief he had expected for his revenge, not even when he heard the news of the family's grieving and witnessed the broken father and the inconsolable mother in the solemn funeral procession and heard how nightly Mrs. Seldorn lashed out at her husband for always forcing their daughter to ride: "She never wanted to ride a horse, but that's the only way she could get your attention. You always fishing and hunting and riding with those nigger boys. She would have done anything to make you happy. I hope you're happy now, you nigger-loving bastard! You killed her, killed her, killed her!" she yelled at him far into the night. Then afterward, Seldorn learned, she refused to say anything to her husband or to allow him to even come into her bedroom. She became the silent childless mother-ghost that Elizabeth had been for a year.

But Seldorn took little of the pleasure he thought he would feel that Danzee knew a parent's grief, that Danzee's marriage, like his own, had been destroyed by this loss, that Danzee's home was empty and full of pain and silence, that Danzee lived with a zombie. No, Seldorn's job was not complete. He could not enjoy the full measure of his revenge until Danzee knew that he, Seldorn, had caused it because he was a man avenging his wife and family.

He awaited his chance.

Slaves, free Negroes, and Whites in Charles City County talked for weeks about the way Seldorn made himself known to Danzee. Everybody agreed the Negro must have lost his mind. It was as if he was asking to be killed. Court was just letting out in Charles City about two months after the accident—which is exactly what everybody had thought it was until this damn fool walked up to Danzee standing there in the Court House yard with about ten other White men—and two or three slaves and a free Negro standing just a few feet away, over where the carriages were lined up. James Seldorn walked right up to Danzee, literally pushing the other White men aside, and declared in a tone so full of quiet rage that nobody could react at first, "I guess you had two months to understand now the pain a parent feels when they lose deir child... What yu sow, dat yu reap."

It was such a simple statement uttered in such a calm voice, and yet so full of venom, that they say Danzee and the other men didn't understand at first—at least not until they looked again into Seldorn's eyes. It was clear then that not only had that nigger killed his daughter, but he wanted the whole world to know it. They couldn't believe he had the gumption.

The Negroes rushed to Elizabeth's house right away to spirit her away to some safe place in the event the White folks wanted to punish her for her husband's foolhardy deed.

James Seldorn's fate, of course, was ordained. No one even considered that there was anything to be done to save him. His bloody body was found a few hours later in the woods three miles from the Court House, where they had dragged it behind a carriage. He had suffered a violent end, but he died knowing that he was not a slave whose family could be taken away from him with no fear of retribution. He lived in a land where men were either free or slaves, and he died to make the point that he, James Seldorn, was a free man.

CHAPTER FOUR

GOD DOES NOT SLEEP

*However long the night may last, there
will be a morning.*

- Proverb

Elizabeth had grown up a motherless child. Now she was a childless mother. When she heard the news that she was also a husbandless wife, she felt a sense of relief that there was nothing else she loved that she could lose.

"Lord knows I been in sorrow's kitchen, and I've licked the pot clean," she declared to the two neighbor women who brought her news of James's death. Having witnessed her mute acceptance of everything that happened to her during the past year, they were stunned by this unexpected declaration. They were further startled at the strength of her voice. But even more surprising was that this silent woman who had barely managed to nod a response to their questions since the Churchmen took her boys away now seemed unable to stop talking. Like a dammed body of water suddenly released, torrents of words flowed without cease.

"I've seen it coming," she declared, looking at them with flashing eyes, eyes that had seemed frozen in a deathly stare so long they had forgotten what a spirited woman Elizabeth had been. "Yes, Lord, I've seen it coming. And I didn't know what to do to stop it. When Josh and Uncle Samuel held him back the night they took John and Abraham, I knew they wouldn't be there to keep holding him forever.

"I could see the determination in his eyes. And ever since then, there's been a kind of waiting, waiting, waiting—like something that he was planning to do—just waiting for the right time. And when he come back in that night before Danzee's girl died, look like he was beginning to feel at peace, like finally, he won't waiting, waiting, waiting no more. Not peace exactly, but like he was **starting** to do whatever it was he'd been waiting to... to do for a little mo'rn a year. It was late at night when he came in tipping, and I say, 'What you tipping for, man, I ain't sleep.'"

"And he laughed, 'cause he was so surprised I said anything, but it was like his mood had took over my spirit too, and I knew something was in the offing.

"'You mus' have some reason for remindin' me that you wake here at fo' o'clock in the morning, woman,' he joked as he cautiously come over to slip in the bed up 'gainst me. Poor man was cautious, 'cause I been just rolling over, turning my back to 'im so long he give up on us loving any more. But we loved that night like we done forgot all that we'd lost. And for the first time since we been married, we didn't worry 'bout no children hearing us. I mean, we had a whole lot o' passion been building up for a whole long time, just waiting for this moment to come flooding out.... Yawl must think I'm terrible talking like this, but me and James pleasured each other till we give pleasure a bad name." Elizabeth laughed, "Yawl, please forgive me for talkin' like this."

"Well, it's not as if we not married women, too," Mary Sue encouraged her to continue.

The dam had burst. She didn't need much encouragement.

"We talked that night like we hadn't talked in a long time. He never told me no details of what he had done; matter of fact, he never told me he'd done anything, and I never asked him. He never mentioned neither anything 'bout what he planned to do. But he said he loved me and Abraham and John and Will more than he loved his own life. He said he was always going to try to protect me and my children as long as he was alive, 'And anybody hurt yawl gon' have to answer to me—one way or another.' Those were his exact words.

"I wanted to beg him not to take any chances, I wanted to explain that I knew a poor colored man didn't have no power against the rich White man and his laws and his lawmen and his Churchmen. But I could tell James was way way past any such talk as that. He was set on a path where he couldn't turn back, and he didn't want to. And I'm shamed to say, I didn't want him to—cause he was noble and powerful in his determination. James had found his manhood. I was so proud of him; I felt a new kind of strength in myself.

"For two months, we were like newlyweds. Couldn't get enough of each other. And always there was that sense that he was moving... moving... moving toward something. He wasn't waiting no more. Something had been started, and its culmination was as inevitable as the landslide when the snow piles up on the mountain, or the hurricane when the winds get started, or the trembling all through my body when he slip that big, throbbing thing o' his 'tween my legs. No need in not wanting it to happen. It was in the works as sure as a promise from God Almighty.

"So, I don't know what James has done, but I know

those White crackers didn't choose the manner of his death. I know he did *all* he had to do, *all* he been waiting to do for more than a year. I know he finished what he started the minute they first come to this house and tore up our family. I know he's at peace, 'cause he said like the Lord, 'Vengeance is mine.' Yes, I'm as sure as I am that I'm standing here before you that whatever happened, my James gave up the ghost like a man and died with a song in his heart."

The women had been so shocked by all this talking from their erstwhile silent friend and so mesmerized by the story she was telling and the pure audacity of it (they would have said sentimentality or romanticism if they had read the novels Elizabeth had on her bookshelves) they almost forgot they had come to take her down in the swamp to hide out at Mama Bess's cabin in case the White folks decided they hadn't spilled enough blood when they killed her husband.

But Elizabeth wasn't hearing about any running away. She was like a minister just getting wound up to make his main point: "This is my home and James's home. He died to let folks know they couldn't just walk into his house and take his children away. How could I live with a man like that and not be brave enough to stay in this house he died for!"

They pleaded and reasoned with her, but Elizabeth wasn't listening. They saw that same kind of look in her gaze that she had seen in James's: "I'm on a mission, and there's no turning back," her flashing eyes signaled.

"I know I can't fight a mob of White men," she calmly conceded to her concerned neighbors, "but, so help me, God, if they step in this yard, I'm gon' try my darndest to put some bullets through a few heads... And I know how to shoot James's rifle," she ended, as if nothing more was to be said on the subject.

"But there is one favor. I want one of you to send somebody with a note to Danzee."

She wrote a simple note, one that reflected the new authority that had been bequeathed to her by her husband:

Dear Mr. Danzee,

I need my sons home with me for a few days.

I expect you know why.

Mrs. Elizabeth Brown Seldorn

The children were home before dark that night. Abraham had been designated to tell her that Mr. Danzee said he was sorry about James's death. He wanted her to know he didn't have anything to do with it.

"Hmmumph," she guffawed. "You don't have to pull the trigger to kill somebody... He killed 'im!"

Abraham, who had presumably been prompted to be sure she understood that Danzee was not responsible, attempted to defend him, but Elizabeth interrupted.

"He is responsible for his death. If he hadn't taken you from us, James wouldn't be dead today. I don't want to hear nothin' else about it!"

Elizabeth enjoyed having her children home for five days. She was surprised at how grown up and independent they had become—poor boys with no mother to take care of them. But they were here now to take care of their mother, and they tried to do the things for her they knew James would have done. They cut wood and brought it in. They filled up all the water jugs so she wouldn't have to go out to the well. They raked the leaves in the yard and put some seeds in for summer vegetables. They even went around making some miscellaneous repairs—putting in a nail here or there. They were learning a lot at Danzee's.

After James' funeral, Elizabeth sent them back to Danzee with another note:

> Dear Mr. Danzee,
> I will need my boys' help around the house now that James is dead. They tell me they don't have to work on Sundays. That would be a good day for them to come home every week.
>
> Mrs. Seldorn

She gave the note to Abraham to give to Danzee, directing him how he was to present and reinforce her case if Danzee appeared reluctant to grant her request. She need not have worried. Danzee said not a word, except to tell Abraham that they could leave an hour before dark every Saturday and come back Sunday night. He even let them take a mule and cart home so that they could take their mother to church on Sunday.

Now that James was gone, Danzee was no longer impelled by jealousy.

Elizabeth was often sad and lonely... and she could

never find it in her heart to forgive Danzee—only a devil could take all her boys away from her and think he was being generous to let them spend one day a week with her. Every time she thought about him, her blood curdled. But she never fell into a depression again. James's spirit reinvigorated her; her boys' visits gave her something to look forward to each week.

She entered into the life of the community again. She worked hard tending her garden, feeding her animals, milking her cows, gathering her eggs, trapping squirrels and rabbits and birds, canning her vegetables, salting her fish, taking in a little sewing to make some spending change.

Danzee subtly sent some little produce and other necessities by the boys.

He felt generous now that James was gone.

Elizabeth lived comfortably.

One by one, as the boys turned twenty-one, Danzee paid them a handsome sum of money for their period of indenture and helped them buy a big plot of land near him. Abraham, an expert carpenter, developed quite a reputation and was soon busy going all over Charles City, New Kent, and even James City, building houses and barns and doing repair work. He kept adding new parcels to the land Danzee had helped him buy until he was the largest colored landowner in the area. He purchased three slaves to do the farming and care for the animals. He married, started a family, built a comfortable house near his own for his mother, and became as much a gentleman farmer and tradesman as a man of color could be in 18th century Virginia.

As John and Will came of age, they also bought parcels of land with Danzee's help. They built houses and married, but they never seemed to take to building a trade or managing a farm the way Abraham had. They preferred to spend their days hunting and fishing, while their land went largely untended, their livestock diminished, and their tools rusted. Both of them kept getting into debt and losing a few acres here and a few acres there. Sometimes Abraham even bought parcels of land from them to provide them money to pay a tax bill or meet some other unanticipated financial exigency.

Then the Revolutionary War came to Virginia. John and Will, seeing the possibility of some excitement, enlisted in the Fourth Virginia Regiment in the fall of 1780. The brothers were thrilled to be soldiers, to be in uniform, to be marching along singing martial songs, to go to North Carolina. The idea of seeing a new state (something their mother, their wives, and most of the colored people they knew had never experienced) was exciting to them. The reality of that new state left much to be desired. North Carolina looked just like Virginia, and life in the army was difficult wherever the troops were; it was pure hell for the colored troops.

Abraham had not been motivated by the same romantic visions as his brothers. But convinced that slavery would be ended if Negroes joined the Colonists in their fight for freedom, Abraham too had marched off with his brothers to North Carolina.

John was killed in the first battle of his unit, the Battle of Guilford Courthouse in North Carolina, and Abraham lost his arm. Will and Abraham came home several months later, angry that their brother had been killed, and they had fought and suffered the hardships of the battlefield for nothing. Life did not improve for Black people. They had fought for the freedom of the White Colonists, and they still did not dare venture beyond their immediate neighborhood without proof of their free status. They who had fought for their nation came back to Charles City where they couldn't even get permission to own a gun—a privilege they had had before they joined the military.[1]

And to make matters even worse, Will's claim for losses of the property taken by his own fellow soldiers who came through Freetown while he was in North Carolina and took over 200 pounds of beef and his one horse was denied. Bitter and depressed, he had finally been killed when a storm caught him and Abraham out on the James and capsized their boat. Abraham had managed to get to shore, but they didn't find Will for a week.

Life had not been easy for Elizabeth, but she found contentment in her old age, surrounded by her grandchildren, Abraham's five, and Will's two (if you count the outside one). Her daughters-in-law were devoted to her, and each seemed to compete for the opportunities to fix her a meal, wash her hair, do whatever little favor they could for their beloved mother.

And her grandchildren. Well, they were the delight of her life. Elizabeth sang and danced with them. She turned rope for them and helped them make balls out of rags and thread. She taught them to read and write, and she told them stories. She helped them dig for worms and sat for hours at the edge of the river's shore fishing with them. She taught them to milk a cow, to gather eggs, to cut up

---

1 A memorial to Patriots of the Revolutionary War stands in Elam Baptist Church Cemetery in Charles City.

a chicken, to set traps for birds and squirrels. They made snowcream and popped corn. She took them to Sunday School and church. She cut hair and braided hair and made dresses and suits. They threaded her needle when she sewed, they held her ball of yarn while she knitted.

Elizabeth was a grandmother with grandchildren. During all the bad times, she had remembered her grandmother's adage, "Wait on the Lord, he'll come in his own time. God does not sleep. God is always on time."

Some days Elizabeth had wondered where God was. Had he forgotten her? He must have been sleeping when those Churchmen rode off with her boys. He must have been asleep when he let those White bastards kill her husband. But now in her old age, she knew her grandmother was right: "They who wait for the Lord shall renew their strength; they shall mount up with wings like eagles; they shall run and not be weary; they shall walk and not faint." (Isaiah 40)

God is good, thank the Lord! Yes, praise his almighty name!

CHAPTER FIVE

A ROSE FOR MR. DANZEE

*Old Man Death don't know the difference
between the big house and the cabin.*
                                    - Slave Proverb

The daughters-in-law, the grands, and their wives, the friends, and neighbors had all finally reluctantly left Elizabeth with her son. Everybody had left, that is, except the two grands, Abraham's youngest daughter—her namesake Liz—and his son, Abraham, Jr. Elizabeth had begged everyone to understand that she was fine, she could get back to the house ok; she didn't need any help, but she wanted—needed—to stay a while longer with this last son she had just buried. To avoid sounding morbid and perhaps making it harder to get rid of them, she didn't add that she wanted to be alone with everybody else who had loved her—her Fa, her Nana, her husband killed by the father of her three sons, and those three sons. To avoid sounding morbid, she didn't say that she herself was ready to stay here in this beautiful old cemetery forever. A mother shouldn't bury all her children. She didn't want to sound melancholic because she really wasn't enduring any emotional trauma. Abraham had suffered a long time, and it was a relief for him and his family to see him close his eyes in peace finally and go to be with his Lord and all the rest of the people Elizabeth was missing more and more.

"You go on now, child," she had insisted first to the daughters-in-law, Martha and Ellen and Patsy, then to her friends Mary and John, to everyone. Her first problem had been her nineteen-year-old grandson, Abraham, Jr., now fancying himself a man and believing he should look out for Elizabeth as his father had. But Elizabeth had been adamant that she be left alone. "It's just so peaceful out here, and the Lord wants me to linger awhile to smell the roses and feel the breeze blow through my hair, and just say my own special prayer for Abraham. You can understand, Junior, I know you can," she turned to one of the last two holdouts. "I'm not no ways upset. My soul is at peace, but I've got some personal praying to do. Go on now, Junior. Go home with your mama," but he wouldn't no more go home without her now than he would most nights that he spent at Elizabeth's house. He had decided before he could talk that he wanted to be with her, and when they tried to take him out of her arms to go home, he just held on to her neck, or her skirt, or her knees or whatever he could grab, and screamed murder if they tried to peel him away. Most folks knew that when he wanted to be with his Nana, it was no need trying to take him away. Today, he didn't even protest that he didn't want to go; he obviously felt no further explanation was necessary than clutching Elizabeth's hand and standing there.

And as Liz looked up into Elizabeth's eyes, they had both laughed out loud, knowing how foolish was the grandmother's prepared speech to this little shadow who was always so close to her that they sometimes literally tripped over one another's foot or slung an arm or a leg over each other in the bed at nights.

But these two grands knew Elizabeth's mood; and when the others had left, they strolled around just far enough away from her for her to ask God if he forgot she was still here, to upbraid God for making her suffer the pain of losing a husband and all three of her sons, one in that Revolutionary War that didn't free nobody but the White folks, one drowned in a storm that capsized his boat in the James, and now Abraham, the strong, handsome, devoted son that survived ten years with a mean and jealous mistress who turned vicious every time she looked into his face and was painfully reminded of her husband's infidelity; Abraham, who survived the Revolutionary War where he lost his left arm, survived that capsized boat where he almost went down with his brother, survived a kidnapping by some slave catchers who tore up his free papers and tried to sell him South, survived all this and came back home to take care of her in her old age and built her a comfortable little shotgun house and a little garden on all that land that he just kept buying up. But for the last year, her beautiful, strong son ... her last son ... he just kept coughing and coughing, tossing and turning all night with a fever that wouldn't break, losing weight till he won't nothing but a skeleton. She tried preparing everything he ever loved to eat to try to tempt him, but no matter how hard he tried, he couldn't seem to get nothing down and keep it there. Soon he was her baby again, so skinny she could turn him over and bathe him and clean his bed without any help from anyone—though his children were always ready to come if she had called. His wife, poor Martha, was so sickly herself she couldn't do much except sit by his bed and try to get him to eat a little something or wipe a little sweat off his brow or fan the flies away. Elizabeth had known then she had to live a while longer to take care of Abraham long as he was on this earth. But why, Lord, why? Why should she stay around now?

Elizabeth had questioned God till she had questioned out, the sun had almost disappeared on the horizon, and the chill in the air reminded her she might as well be going home. Abraham, Jr., and Liz had wandered so far she had almost forgotten she was not alone, but they had not forgotten her. They immediately responded to the subtle change in her demeanor, signaling that she and the Lord were finished their talk for the day.

Sprinting to her side, neither said a word, but each gave her a big hug and grabbed one of her hands. They all stood for another moment, looking down at Abraham's fresh grave and uttered a silent prayer. Elizabeth picked up a couple of the loose flowers spread over his grave, and the three turned to go home.

As they left the familiar graves, Liz pointed over to another section of the cemetery, one with big mausoleums, a section in which she had roamed while her grandmother communed. "Who was William Joseph Danzee?" she asked. "And why does he have such a big vault?"

Elizabeth was surprised at her own calm response. "He was one o' the big White plantation owners here."

All those years since he had taken her sons from her and then had her husband killed, she had hated Danzee so bitterly that if she so much as heard his name mentioned, she just about lost her religion and her home training and could only rant and rave and damn his soul to hell. When that devil Danzee was dying alone in his big house ten years ago, just before the boys went off to fight in the war, Abraham had told her he was begging for her to come and take care of him or at least visit him and say she forgave him. All she could do was roll her eyes, suck her teeth, and spit.

Abraham, understanding his mother's anger, but also

determined to give his all to his father's final request, had even tried to soften her heart. "Mama, I know how he hurt you, but he's dying now. He couldn't never really take us away from you, and he did try to do everything he could to help us—he educated us, taught us trades, sold us land, gave us money. And, mama, he never stopped loving you. He always used to tell us the only time he was happy was when he was in our house with you and us...."

Her scowl ended Abraham's plea.

"I understand, mama," he had relented... And the conversation was ended for eternity.

"Why ain't there no more Danzees around here?" Liz persisted. "Didn't Mr. Danzee have no children?"

"Well, you eleven now and so I guess it's 'bout time you knew. Yeah, Mr. Danzee had one daughter where got killed cause o' his meanness, and the only sons he had—well, they was by me."

Elizabeth didn't look to see how her grand was taking this news. She just tightened her hand a bit around hers.

"Yes, he was your grandpa, but he was White, so he couldn't never say your daddy and his brothers was his sons.... He loved 'em, though." She couldn't believe the compassionate tone she heard in her own voice. "He took them to live with him and took care of them and educated them and taught them a trade. Sometimes he let them ride with him to Richmond and Williamsburg. He even took your daddy with him to New York once, and they went to a theater."

Elizabeth was surprised she wasn't telling them about the pain she felt when he took her children from her—that knife in her heart that still throbbed, that emptiness in her loins that still ached. But somehow, now looking down at these big, stony vaults that held all there ever was of the

Danzees—husband, wife, and daughter—her anger just fizzled away as she held the warm hands of her beautiful grandchildren, William Joseph Danzee's beautiful grandchildren whom he never got a chance to hold.

"Poor man," Liz commiserated. "How sad and lonely he must have been."

"Why would you feel sorry for a slaveholding White man?" Elizabeth demanded in shock at her namesake's misplaced sympathy.

"Why, look at them there, covered with all that cold stone, and no one to visit their grave and cut the weeds away or plant a rose bush or say a little prayer. And he could never live with his sons... or love them, like daddy loved us. Can owning slaves and living in a big plantation house make you as happy as we are loving our family?"

"Poor man," Liz repeated, finally breaking the silence that echoed after her last long speech.

Suddenly Liz dashed back to her father's grave and slipped a few of his many flowers away. Returning to the mausoleum that held the Danzees, she tenderly laid the flowers down and softly repeated, "Poor man."

Elizabeth, rich in the love of her family, felt the last bit of hatred toward her White paramour and mother dissolve. "A little child shall lead them," she thought, as she took one of her roses and pulled two petals off, silently blessing the spirits of the William Joseph Danzee who had loved her and fathered her children, and of the beautiful Moll who had given birth to her and taught her to read, Moll, who had died without ever knowing about her grands and great-grands.

"Poor Mr. Danzee... Poor Moll," she whispered as a tear rolled down her cheek. White folks got so tied up in their own rules about race that despite all their power, they weren't free no how. Shut up in that big old mansion with a family he despised; now entombed in all this granite, Danzee never knew the freedom and happiness and love Elizabeth had with her Fa and Nana, with James, with her sons and grandsons. What the White folks robbed her of was small compared to what they cheated themselves out of.

Freed of the burden of her anger and hatred, Elizabeth took her grandchildren's hands and headed back to what was left of her family.

CHAPTER SIX

ABRAHAM'S LEGACY

*What White folks don't know won't hurt
them, but what they know sure will hurt
us.*

- Abraham to his children

braham Brown, Jr., turned twenty-one on July 4,
1792, at which time he came into his inheritance.
He was the heir to a small fortune for a Negro in
Charles City, Virginia. His father, who died in 1790, had
bequeathed Abraham, Jr., the lion's share of his exten-
sive land holdings (400-plus acres), and his mother, who
died in 1791, had also shown extreme partiality toward
this favored first-born, leaving him her Bay Horse Colt
and Silvy, the Negro woman who had been owned by the
family ever since Abraham, Jr., was a toddler. His father
had purchased her and her child Sal when his brother Will
confirmed the rumors spreading around Freetown that he
was the child's father. Abraham, who had lived on a slave
plantation as an indentured servant, could not allow his
niece to remain a slave—and the owner of Pleasant Grove
Plantation made the most of his opportunity to realize a
juicy profit. Abraham knew he was being overcharged, but
when the mercenary slave master started talking about
what a "pretty lil honey-brown gal like Sal would fetch in
a few years," he knew he would kill the venal bastard if

he said another word. He almost flung the money at the chuckling miscreant and fled home with Sylvy and her little girl.

Will's wife was not in a mood to welcome her husband's outside woman and their bastard child into their home, and so Silvy and Sal had remained with Abraham and Sarah. During the ensuing years, Sarah and Silvy became close friends, a bond that further eroded Sarah's already tenuous relationship with her sister-in-law, who never set foot in their home after Sylvy arrived. Abraham, Jr., was raised to treat Sylvy with the respect due a member of the family and to protect her and Sal from any possibility of re-enslavement. As much as she would have missed Sylvy, Sarah had always wanted to send her and her child to the North where they could be free, a desire about which she became even more determined as her own health deteriorated, but Sylvy insisted on staying in Charles City near her other children, who were slaves on Pleasant Grove Plantation. The laws of Virginia, of course, did not allow freed slaves to remain in the state, so, for their own security, Sylvy and Sal had to remain the property of Abraham and Sarah. The best protection the dying Sarah could offer her was to will her to her son, Abraham, Jr. He had already inherited Sal from his father's will.

In addition to the slaves and land, Abraham, Jr., and his siblings had also come into a considerable bit of money—not mentioned in the will for fear that the White folks at the Courthouse might conspire to cheat them out of it—no matter what the will said. They had all later laughed at the stipulation in the will "bequest[ing] to my loving wife Sarah Brown twenty-five pounds ...," precisely the amount Abraham kept in his chest for any of the authorities to see. They remembered Abraham's laughing maxim, "What White folks don't know won't hurt them, but what they know sure will hurt us."

Abraham—and most other free Negroes—knew all too well how often Whites ignored or nullified wills and stole the hard-earned money and land intended for Negro beneficiaries. Abraham and his brothers had themselves been cheated out of everything Mr. Danzee had willed to them by some "relatives" who turned up as soon as he died and contested his will. But they had learned from Danzee not to trust the legal system to carry out one's last will and testimony, especially insofar as colored heirs were concerned. Danzee had not only transferred titles to some land to them while he was alive, but he had also instructed them to quickly take away the silver and animals and cash and even crops before the arrival of the relatives, who had taken great care not to come until Danzee was beyond the need for nursing care.

Thus, each of Abraham's five children knew one of the three hiding places where Abraham stashed away his cash—three places so that if one child were ever forced to reveal where money was hidden, he couldn't compromise all of Abraham's hoard. And they had all been directed that in case of any threat from the White folks after their father's death, they were to divide the money, secure their documents certifying their free status, and set out for Canada. Each child had drilled into him the names and addresses of individuals who would help them on that journey in strategically placed homes in Washington, Baltimore, Philadelphia, New York, and Boston. They were made to recite those names and addresses like they recited the alphabet and the times table when they did their lessons. Abraham and his family were free Blacks and free Blacks of some means, but they lived each day in preparation for the moment that that freedom might be threatened, and the dark night of slavery seemed about to engulf them. "A-B-C-D-E-F-G ... ought times two is ought, one times two is two, two times two is four; three times two is six.... In Washington, inquire for Mr. Robert Emanuel, who lives on the Northeast corner of 14th Street at the intersection with _____ Street. In Baltimore, ask for Mr. and Mrs. George Jefferson, who live..."

They were constantly reminded, "Mind how you talk. Bush have ears."

Twenty-one-year-old Abraham, Jr., did not feel like the young, carefree lord of a large estate. The land and the money and the animals and the slaves had not been his major legacy. His most important legacy was the lessons his father had hammered into his mind and soul for as long as he could remember. "Never forget that you live in a land of slaves, and as long as there are slaves and you are a member of that race of slaves, at any moment, you can lose your freedom." He grew up hearing how Abraham and John and Will had been seized from their mother and apprenticed to Mr. Danzee. And even though they were lucky that Danzee was their father and even loved them, what happened to them was a reminder that any White man might take the children of free Blacks away at any moment. And it wasn't only the children that were at risk. Fail to pay your taxes, and they could sell you as a slave. Be accused of a crime, and they could sell you as a slave. Get caught with a gun without a proper permit, get caught on the river without authorization, get caught on the road without your papers, and you could be enslaved.

Die without a will, and your own "slaves" reverted back to the state. Abraham, Jr. knew the burden and the dangers of being a free Negro, and he had been relentlessly tutored in his responsibility for his siblings, his mother, his grand-mother, and his slaves if his daddy should die.

He had also been carefully tutored to read and write and do numbers. He was taught that if he couldn't read and write, he might as well just wrap his land up and hand it over to the first White man who came along. He was taught that if he couldn't count and figure, he might as well hand his money over to the first White man that came along and say, "Here, take what you want." Abraham, Jr. was carefully taught all of his father's trades and the value of the ownership of land. A thief could steal your money, and you'd never see it again, but land was safe wealth, which no one could slip off with in the night. Put 96 pounds in your chest, and next year when you take it out, you've still got 96 pounds. But take that 96 pounds, as Abraham did in 1769, and buy 155 acres of land; then sell wood off it, raise crops on it, feed animals on it, and next year you'll have the land and 96 more pounds you made off it. Plus, you can have a leg of venison or a roast wild turkey or a stuffed shad or a baked sturgeon on your table every day of the year according to the seasons. Your land will provide you with vegetables and fruits and nuts. It wasn't easy for a free Negro to make money in a land of slaves where scores of laws proscribed what he could do, but Abraham had taught his son the value of owning land, knowing a trade, and just plain hard work; and by the time his father died, Abraham, Jr., knew a thousand ways to earn a pound and invest it so that it would grow. He never forgot, however, that his father warned him he must never advance his own fortunes from the evil of slavery. He might legally own slaves, but he must never make a cent off the enforced labor of others. They must be paid for whatever labor they did, and they and their children should be given their freedom whenever they wished it.

Abraham, Jr., was also carefully schooled not to indulge in behavior that might incur the wrath of White men. "Get, but don't make a show of what you have," his father preached. "Don't build a big house out where they see it whenever they pass and compare it with their own." His father had built his house way back in the woods and, even then, had been careful not to make it too ostentatious, though he was the best carpenter in the county and could have afforded a splendid residence. "Don't ride about in too fine a carriage. Don't dress in clothes that make you stand out. Don't speak the King's English your grandmother taught you in the presence of White people—a little plantation speech is safer. Don't do anything that will call attention to yourself or arouse their anger, jealousy, or vindictiveness. If anyone seems to be annoyed with you, apologize profusely, smile vacuously, play the humble nigger. Always try to control your temper and walk away from any confrontation... But if you can't escape their wrath, and you can't avoid attack, take some of the bastards with you! Try to live in this world, but if you must die, then die like a man who came from a line of soldiers who fought in the Revolutionary War for somebody's freedom. Die like a man from a family that shed its own blood and cut down a few British soldiers so this nation could be free." (In his teaching mode, Abraham spoke in the proper English in which Elizabeth had drilled him. In other circumstances, he would drift into varying degrees of the slow, relaxed Virginia drawl or even the broken pidgin speech that reinforced his White countrymen's sense of their superiority.)

No, Abraham, Jr., would never know what it meant to be a carefree youth. For as long as he could remember, he was being groomed and tutored in the art of survival and warned of all the traps waiting to ensnare him. Many was the night he awoke dreaming he was being dragged away in chains in a long line of shackled Negroes to be sold in the South. He always woke up when the slave-trader, mad that young Abraham wouldn't stop screaming that he was free, lashed him with the whip. He woke up feeling the sting of that whip on his back and would often reach around to rub "the injury" during the day, so real was the sense of the lingering pain of that blow.

No, Abraham, Jr., never had the leisure for a carefree youth. He was a man with grave responsibilities who lived in enemy territory, and he had been groomed all of his life to fight to maintain and protect his family and himself.

On the morning of his birthday, July 4, 1792, Abraham, Jr., rounding a curve, his mind all cluttered with thoughts of everything except the present moment, looked up in surprise as the Charles City Courthouse appeared like a mirage. He quickly pulled himself together, dismounted, and walked over to join Mr. Turner Southall and Mr. Major Willcox, executors of his father's will, and Mr. James Parrish, executor of his mother's will. The presence of these respected White gentlemen helped to facilitate a smooth transferal of titles to the slave and land that he had inherited. His father had carefully cultivated the "friendship" of these White citizens to protect his family against any seizure of his estate. He had already paid them well, but Abraham, Jr., expressed his gratitude through lavish gifts of smoked hams and pear preserves and pickled cucumbers. He also assured them that if they needed any carpenter work done, they should simply send a messenger to summons him. He smiled and "yassuhd" and "Thankyuh, suhd" them until he thought he would puke. The men smiled, patted him on the back, and wished him well.

With his papers in his saddlebag within a few hours, Abraham, Jr., experienced an unaccustomed sense of relief and security. He felt like singing as he jumped on his mother's bay horse and galloped home to share the good news with his family, who could now relax. Their estate was secure.

Elizabeth's heart swelled with pride as she witnessed her handsome grandson so masterfully claim his inheritance and take over his parents' comfortable home with all the responsibility of younger siblings and slaves and, yes, his "poor old feeble grandma." These were the words she used to describe herself, but Elizabeth at seventy-five, having outlived her husband, the father of her sons, and those three sons, was still a strong and straight and mentally alert woman. She refused to even listen to her grandson's pleas that she move out of the little shotgun house her son Abraham had built her and live with them in the big house, also built by her son Abraham. And though there were always grands coming by to do things for her, she cooked her own food (still on the stove Danzee gave her), churned her own butter, made her own clothes, knitted seine for the men to fish (Abraham, Jr., and his father before him wouldn't go out during shad season with seine made by anybody except Elizabeth), and piddled around a bit in her garden;... and right now she was piecing together a pink and white baby quilt for her first great-grand.

Yes, Abraham, Jr., and his wife, Susannah, were expecting, and from the way Susannah was carrying that child, Elizabeth knew it was gon' be a little girl.

Elizabeth had been so happy when Abraham, Jr., had decided to get married, though she had refused to be a party to the schemes of all those mothers of marriageable girls in Freetown who were always plotting to get to him through her—bringing her canned fruits and knitting her shawls and just happening to bring their daughters along with them when they delivered them—asking her to dinner and telling her to get young Abraham to bring her. "Why, Nancy," she had facetiously replied to one neighbor, "what difference does it make who brings me—if I'm the one you're inviting to dinner? Matter of fact, I can walk that little distance."

Nancy's cheeks had reddened, but she was up to the challenge. She looked her straight in the eyes without trying to hide her motives: "Elizabeth, why would you walk through all those muddy lanes when you've got that handsome young grandson with a carriage. Why not bring him along? I'm sure he would enjoy the company of my youngans."

Finally, Nancy, Susanna's mother, had won, but not through no female schemes. Her husband, Bill, and Abraham, Jr., started driving to Richmond together to sell their produce, and they started going fishing together, and they started helping each other out at crop-gathering season or hog-killing time—much like Bill and the Abraham that was now dead had done. As an old friend of the father, and as a man who had no son of his own, it was natural that he would step in and become a fatherly companion to Abraham, Jr. And Susannah's mother always found some way to capitalize on this relationship in order to give Abraham, Jr., a look at her charming daughter. Susannah would be sent to answer the door whenever he came to pick up her papa, or she would run out with a basket of eggs to be sold just when they were about to drive off to Richmond, or she would appear with a lunch for them when they were fishing from the shore, or she would keep the pots boiling when it was hog-killing time. Soon, knowing what a sweet tooth Abraham, Jr. had, she began preparing a little packet (fresh fruit cobbler or chocolate cake or bread pudding) for him to take home "in case you get hungry at night." Abraham, Jr. didn't stand a chance and never suspected till they got married that it was her mother baking all those goodies, and Susannah couldn't cook worth a darn. But he was in love by that time and swore it didn't matter. And I guess it didn't since they could go by her parents whenever they wanted for meals. Bill and Nancy would do anything to encourage the young couple's visits, so thrilled were they that their daughter had won the prize trophy in Freetown, and so lonely were they without their only child.

And Abraham, Jr., was pretty happy too—not only did he have a smart yellow gal with a pretty smile and long, straight hair, but he had parents again. This was a deal made in heaven, and even the death of Elizabeth one year and one day after the baby's birth did not cast gloom on this happy household.

Elizabeth had been so delighted with her pretty great-granddaughter Polly that she had simply moved into Abraham's house. No one ever acknowledged the move, but from the day Polly was born, she never again slept in her own house. Bit by bit, her clothes and pots and pans and pictures and keepsakes and books found their way to the big sunny room next to the room where Abraham, Jr., and Susanna slept with Polly. Elizabeth did everything for Polly except breastfeeding her. She sang to her and told her stories; she read the Bible to her; she sat in the porch glider and rocked her to sleep. She sometimes called the spirits to come see her, "Abraham, look at pretty, pretty Polly. Polly, give a big smile to your granddaddy," she would command, and Polly would look and smile as if she too recognized his presence. Then she would tell her to kiss her step great-granddaddy James, and Polly would purse her lips to this visitor as well. Elizabeth's happiness made her generous enough to even invite Danzee and Moll to witness the latest in their line, and little Polly would squeal with joy at all the visitors "come to our party" (Elizabeth would say), all carefree and loving now that they were freed of the awkward constraints and demands of this world with its race and class divisions. Though Elizabeth died the day after Polly's first birthday, Polly always swore, to the amazement of everyone, that she could remember these parties. She could even describe in detail all those spirits who visited her. They never came again after Elizabeth's death, but Polly's love for her grands would be expressed in the tales that she would share with her children, born many years (but perhaps not enough years) afterward.

Polly also always thereafter experienced a day of solitude the day after her birthday. She never seemed to anticipate it or to prepare anyone for it, but that day she always spent alone in her bed. Neither the cries of children nor the demands of adults elicited any response to her. She just lay there as if in a coma, hugging the quilt Elizabeth made. She did not mourn or cry; it was as if she were in some deep and peaceful reverie that neither sibling nor parent could penetrate. The following day, she would be herself again, rising early to start her regular routine as a mother/daughter/hard-working woman.

Elizabeth had planned for Polly's first birthday for weeks. She painted a beautiful birthday card, made an exquisite pink dress with matching underskirt and ribbon, baked a cake, and made ice cream. They ate and sang and played until both great-grand and baby fell asleep on the living room rug. Susannah picked Polly up to put her to bed, and Abraham, Jr., tried to arouse his grandmother. She smiled at him so sleepily that he simply picked her up and carried her to her bed. He attributed the fact that she could not be fully aroused to nothing more serious than exhaustion arising from her exertion for the last few days. He did something he had never had to do for her before; he tenderly removed her clothes and slipped her nightgown over her head, recalling the way he and Elizabeth had tended his dying dad, though it never once occurred to him that she was expiring. As he tucked the quilts around her neck and leaned down to kiss her forehead, she smiled wearily and whispered, "Goodnight, son."

When Elizabeth did not respond to Polly's first cries the next morning, Abraham, Jr., and Susannah rushed to her room. She lay motionless, but she opened her eyes when Polly started clambering up on her bed. As Polly reached over to kiss her great-gran's cheek, Elizabeth seemed to whisper something into the child's ear. Polly squealed with delight, sat up, looked around, and offered kisses to some visitors that apparently only she and the dying woman could see. As a faint smile flickered on Elizabeth's lips, she gasped and was no more.

Abraham and Susannah starred down at the supine, Elizabeth. Only Polly looked up and saw her great-grand lifted tenderly in the arms of Death as he mounted his horse and rode off beyond the horizon. Polly would never forget the vision she had of a sublime and youthful Elizabeth happily relaxing in the arms of her divine rescuer. Thenceforth, Polly knew that death was not a fate to be feared, but the beginning of a new life.

Thereafter Polly would not go to sleep without her pink and white quilt. When she, herself, became a mother, her three children would be put to bed under that quilt. She had given it to each of those children in turn as they had children, to be used, she dictated until the next great-grand came. But at some point, Elizabeth's quilt was lost, and everyone pointed the finger at everyone else as the one who last had the quilt. By this time, however, Polly was almost as old as the Elizabeth she remembered, and she no longer needed a quilt to remember her grandmother; she had long since learned to spend her day of solitude without it. She would soon be going to join Elizabeth and all those other grands whose "visits" she had enjoyed so much as a child. Earthly treasures no longer mattered. She even listed to hear the divine horseman galloping to rescue her: "Lord, I want to cross over into campground."

CHAPTER SEVEN

THE SEED OF ABRAHAM

And the Lord appeared unto Abram, and said, "Unto thy seed will I give this land;" and there builded he an altar unto the Lord, who appeared unto him.

- Genesis 12:7

And the Lord multiplied the seed of Abraham as the stars of the heaven and as the sand which is upon the seashore. Abraham (he had dropped the junior after his grandmother's death), and Susanna had eleven children. God blessed them with good health and modest wealth. The only thing that could have made their lives happier was freedom, something they had less and less of with each passing year.

Every session, the Virginia Assembly passed new laws designed expressly to limit the rights of free Negroes and to make it more and more difficult for them to make a living. Free Negroes now had to register periodically and obtain a certificate confirming they were free. The Assembly made it illegal for free Negroes to own more than one gun and passed varied laws limiting the movement of Negroes in other jurisdictions than the one in which they were registered and on waterways. Richmond even forbade Negroes to ride in carriages other than in the capacity of servant or coachman. Still more disturbing were those laws establishing greater and greater penalties for any infraction that might be interpreted as inciting slaves to rebel or escape.

Abraham and Susanna often talked about moving their family to Canada where they could truly be free, but with each passing year, their land and wealth grew, and they knew it would be well-nigh impossible to start over again in a new country with eleven children.

So, Abraham struggled and connived to continue his businesses despite the laws. Instead of taking his produce to Richmond in his comfortable gig, he and one of his sons rode his horses, pulling a loaded cart. He was constantly paying bribes to get special permits to own and operate his boats and to ply his trades.

But he and Susanna never breathed freely until night-time when they and all eleven children were safe under their roof. The older the children became, the more their apprehension increased. There was always the fear the boys might stray to some forbidden area, they might pick up some forbidden paper or journal, they might lose their free papers, they might become involved in some altercation with a White boy, they might be entrapped or kidnapped.

And once the girls started blooming into womanhood, they were never allowed to go out on the roads alone lest they be molested by any White man who chose to do so. No laws protected the virtue of colored women; there was no such thing as the rape of a colored woman. In effect, there was no such thing as a crime against a colored person, since they could not testify against Whites in court.

Incident after incident drove Abraham to the end of his rope. First, his son Samuel was kidnapped right off the road in front of their home by slave dealers. Major, who saw the whole incident, had been smart enough to follow them furtively. As soon as he saw that his brother Samuel was taken to the Hill plantation, he hightailed it home to inform his dad. Abraham quickly gathered together a few courageous friends, and they rode off with their guns, hopeful the whole incident could be settled peacefully but determined to free Samuel with force if that were necessary—come what may. The members of this free community bent over backward to follow the letter of the law and to appease their White neighbors, but there was an unspoken resolution (and the White community knew this) that there would be bloodshed if anyone attempted to enslave their children.

When Abraham and his friends rode up to the plantation house, Hill himself was in the front yard with the slave-traders, and Samuel was chained to three slaves Hill was selling. A murderous fury seized Abraham when he saw his son a part of a slave coffle. He forgot all the protocol of Black/White interactions and raced up so fast that Hill jumped back lest he be trampled:

"That's my *son* chained there! What the hell is going on?" he yelled.

"Your son?" Hill feigned surprised. "I, uh, uh... thought this was, uh, uh... someone these gentlemen bought on t-t-their way here."

The three traders, still startled by the angry colored men with the rifles, did not even attempt to justify their behavior, but quickly released the panicked boy.

Samuel later told his father that the traders had torn up his free papers when he proffered them to verify his status. He then declared that he had loudly appealed to Mr. Hill, clearly identifying himself as Abraham's son, but Hill had ignored him and seemed quite willing to have him taken off with the slaves he was selling—until Abraham appeared.

Abraham was furious, but he realized he was lucky he had caught the blasted slave-traders and that they had not put up a fight. There was no winning for a Black man in a situation that turned violent. He could get a replacement of Samuel's free papers. His son was safe.

Not so, the other slaves, whom Abraham knew and who were being sold away from their families. Abraham had wanted to break their chains and whisk them away as well, but it would have been a foolhardy act that would only end up in his imprisonment or even execution. He would send Susanna over tonight to comfort the wives and daughters and give them a fresh ham. A guilt offering. He felt he was a coward. But what could he do? He knew the laws. He knew the courts. He knew the jails.

Indeed, Abraham had recently been hauled into court when he was discovered with a copy of *The Interesting Narrative of the Life of Olaudah Equiano, or Gustavus Vassa, the African*. He had had to spend all the money he got from his corn crop that year to hire a lawyer to defend him against the charge that he "had knowingly and feloniously circulated the *Narrative*..., a libelous and false account of slavery published in New York of an incendiary character with intent in so doing to advise and incite Negroes in the state to rebel or make insurrection or to inculcate resistances to the right of property of masters in their slaves." Abraham claimed he had picked the book up from curiosity when he saw it lying in the marketplace in Richmond. In truth, he purchased it from an acquaintance in Richmond who sold copies of slave narratives and other antislavery material that he smuggled into the state. The lawyer argued that Abraham was a stupid nigger who couldn't even read well enough to know what the book was all about. White friends offered testimony of Abraham's good character and expressed doubt that he understood the actual content of the book he had in his possession. Abraham was ultimately exonerated, but not until he had spent countless sleepless nights in a cold, damp jail, wondering what would become of his family if he were convicted. Then when he was at last acquitted, instead of feeling great relief, Abraham had an inexplicable compulsion to get his book back. It was insane, he knew, but he hated to lose the one book he had ever read about a Negro. The loss of the book made him even angrier than the trial. His lawyer almost literally kicked him out of his office when Abraham asked after the trial if he couldn't make an effort to get his book back.

The end of the line for Abraham came one Saturday morning in 1801 when he was accosted by some poor crackers outside of Richmond and had his wagon of produce and his free papers, not to mention his wallet, stolen from him. The thieves had intended to kidnap him, but as two of the foolish men examined their loot, Abraham saw his chance to escape from the third, who thought he had tied him securely to the back of the cart. Abraham, who had held his hands in such a way that there was considerable slackness in the knot, kicked his guard in his private parts, and, before the others could react, he snatched his hands free and dashed off into the woods. As the two able-bodied rascals started after him, Abraham pelted them with a few well-chosen rocks that soon sent them scurrying back to their cohort, who was still rolling on the ground, shamelessly holding his wounded "jewels" and whimpering.

Abraham's walk back to Charles City took eight hours because he had to stay in the woods lest he be arrested as a runaway slave. It was not difficult to renew his free papers once he got to the Courthouse, but the incident had driven him to the point of no return. It was impossible to press charges against the thieves; indeed, had he been foolish enough to try, he, himself, would have been prosecuted for the felony of kicking and injuring White men. The law declared that "if any Negro, mulatto, or Indian, bond or free, shall at any time lift his or her hand in opposition against any Christian, not being Negro, mulatto, or Indian, he or she so offending, shall for every such offense... receive on his or her bare back thirty lashes, well laid on."[1]

He had lost two horses, a cart, and several pounds worth of produce to worthless scoundrels, and there was no recourse for him. Added to the money he spent defending himself because he bought a book, these losses meant he had worked these first ten months of the year only to hand over his profits to his enemies. There was no way now he could buy the gold watch he had planned as a surprise for Susanna for Christmas and for which he had put aside a few coins every time he went to Richmond. There was no way he could purchase the little piece of property he was looking to buy. His labor lined the pockets of White men. He was little more than their slave!

On his walk back home, he had come to a decision to join four other friends of his in Southhampton who were plotting a rebellion. They had discreetly contacted him some months before with their plan, which was to have a captain in every county to organize slaves and free Negroes who could be trusted; at midnight on December 25, 1801, they would set fire to the homes of the slaveowners and cut the Whites down with sickles or rifles as they attempt-

---

1 1705 law. Reiterated in 1748. A 1792 law repeats the same punishment but does, for the first time, make an exception for a "Negro [who] was wantonly assaulted and lifted his hand in self-defense."

ed to exit. Slaves, always off for Christmas day, would be free to pass the word and work on their plans throughout the day. This would be the ideal time to surprise the White community, who would be exhausted from the festivities of the holidays. They wanted Abraham to be their captain in Charles City.

For the next three months, Abraham had agonized over the plan. It offered some possibility of some success, but frankly, he was afraid. At any moment, just one traitor could jeopardize all of their carefully plotted rebellion, and all of their heads would roll. Would the slaves sacrifice their celebration at Christmas to stay sober and prepare for war? Even if everything went according to plan and they succeeded in freeing the slaves in Virginia, wouldn't other states send troops as soon as they heard of the uprising? Would the Federal Government send soldiers to suppress them? Was there any way they could defeat a nation?

But after he was robbed, Abraham knew that no matter what the consequence, he could no longer survive under his present conditions. He would never be truly free in a land where his fellows were slaves. He would never be free in a land where there were no laws to protect him and no courts where he had a voice.

The following Saturday, Abraham packed his new cart with preserves, cider, dried fruit, and salted fish, so that if he were questioned, he could claim he was going to sell his produce. He had carefully instructed Susanna that if she didn't hear from him in thirty days, she was to pack the family and head for Canada. She and his children knew the safe houses to stop along the way, and she should leave a message at a selected home in Canada to let him know how and where to find her if he were ever able to join her there. She was to take all the carefully hidden money, except one small bundle Abraham buried in the woods behind their house—the same brown leather pouch his great-grandfather Abraham had kept for his grandmother Elizabeth's escape, and his father Abraham had used for a similar purpose.

Confident that his family could escape, even if he were discovered and killed, Abraham set off for the rendezvous at dawn on a cold November day. He made the two-day drive to Southhampton in less than eighteen hours, but he still arrived later than the others, who had quietly gathered in the woods behind the house of Amos Ricks, who had moved to Southampton three years ago from Charles City's Freetown when his wife inherited her parents' farm.

As Abraham rode into the yard of the house, the plotters were being herded out of the woods by several gun-toting White men. He had always considered the possibility of discovery and capture, but it had never seemed possible that after riding all these hours, he would never even get a chance to speak with his fellow conspirators... Abraham's stomach sank, his heart pounded. What should he do? To try to escape would arouse suspicion of involvement; to stay... well, to stay would mean that he would be rounded up with the others. Suddenly, he realized his best chance was to escape, but his hesitation had been fatal. By the time he turned his cart around, they were upon him. He was seized and hauled off to jail with the rest of the men.

The other captives showed no signs of recognizing him so that when they were taken to court the next day, he was released, there being, the court found, "Insufficient evidence appearing against this prisoner" who was initially charged, like the others, with "plotting and conspiring with others to murder the white people of this county."[2] His tale that he had driven to the house to seek directions to the marketplace where he could sell his goods was believed.

He never discovered what had exposed their plot before it could get started, and he dared not communicate with his fellow conspirators, lest he face some further accusations.

Abraham's terrifying encounter put the fear of the Lord in him. He knew how close he had come to being executed and perhaps having his body quartered and displayed. He could not explain the fact that he (and the fellow plotters, as well, he later learned) had been exonerated—all of them. Usually, in these instances, charges would be pressed anyway, just to make an example of Negroes who allowed themselves to even be suspected of plotting. In this instance, though, no one of the accused could be brought to admit any guilt or point any finger.

Abraham realized God had spared him for some special mission. On his journey home, he had three visions of the Lord appearing to him.

In the most vivid manifestation, Abraham had fallen asleep in the woods when he had stopped to have a bite to eat. He dreamed he was walking along when suddenly he saw his head mounted on a post. He looked into the forlorn eyes of the skull, and they both started to cry, but then Abraham realized he could shed no tears because he had no head. He had been decapitated! Confused and frightened, he reached toward his skull to retrieve it, but it

---

2 Quotations are from the Southampton County Minute Book 1799-1803.

was up too high. Three times, he tried to reclaim his weeping head, but each time he fell far short of the mark. He was powerless to put himself back together again.

He fell to the ground, his body jerking around like a just-beheaded chicken.

And then, God called his name. "Abraham." It was spoken clearly and precisely, not loud, but distinctly audible—and authoritative—like a patient mother issuing an order to her child who had just been on the brink of committing some bad deed. Abraham looked up and beheld a ray of light brighter than anything he had ever seen—far brighter even than the sun. In the midst of the light, there appeared a heavenly figure standing above him, holding his head out to him as if he were offering the cup of salvation. Not even trembling now, so comforting was his vision, Abraham stood up, and God placed his head back on his shoulders. Abraham felt a rapture too deep for words. A joy and peace that he had never fathomed filled his soul. He fell to his knees, crying holy, holy, into the Lord. "Thank you, Lord! Thank you, Jesus. Thank you, God Almighty. I know you spared my life for a reason. Guide me. Direct me. Thy will be done. I shall never fail to praise your name and do your work!"

And then he heard singing that filled him as though some holy gospel sounds radiated from his very belly: "I know the Lord, I know the Lord-d-d, I know the Lord has laid his hands on me." The sounds echoed through the woods and first raised him up and then flung him down in drained ecstasy.

Abraham lay prostrate on the ground. He knew not how long he remained there, but while he was thus engulfed in the light of the Holy Ghost, his soul ascended to the skies; he looked up and saw himself in the presence of the Great God Almighty. And there on the earth, his empty frame shuddered when God spoke to the soul that stood before his throne: "By grace, you are saved. Heed my words henceforth. This is the task I have set you to do."

Abraham pulled his team out on the road. For the first time since he had left home, he felt the sun warm on his face. Birds sang. A rabbit dashed across the road in front of him, then turned, looked at Abraham, rose on his hind feet, and lifted his paws up as if to greet the traveler. Abraham smiled. He looked ahead and saw a world of fall trees, all golden and orange, and magenta. At the end of a large field of wheat, a family of magnificent deer, their large ears erect, the males' proud antlers framing the horizon, seemed to salute the passerby. This land had a life of its own—despite the meanness of slavery and racism. Abraham shook the reins, laid on the whip, and yelled "Y-I-A-A-H, G-I-T-T-T-T-U-P-P!" hurrying his team into a faster trot—eager now to get home to his family. "Y-I-A-A-H, G-I-T-T-T-T-U-P-P!"

When Abraham arrived back in Charles City, safe and sound and whole, he immediately set out to accomplish the special job that the Lord had called him to do. He would start a church for his colored brethren in the midst of the land of slavery.

For the next eight years, he preached the word of the Lord in a little log structure he erected in the same place where he had often gone with his grandmother Elizabeth when he was a boy. In 1809 three preachers from Petersburg came to Freetown to carry on a revival of sorts. During that experience, Abraham realized that he had much to learn in order to properly establish a true church. So he started going to services each Sunday to a colored church in Petersburg. It was a long and arduous trip, but he and his family, and a few of his neighbors, started their preparations long before the light of day, drove their buggy the four miles to the James River, and then rowed eight miles across the James and twelve miles up the Appomattox River to their destination in Petersburg. There they listened to moving sermons, prayed devout prayers, and lifted their voices in song:

> I don't feel weary and noways tired,
> O glory hallelujah
> Just let me in the kingdom while the world
> Is all on fire,
> O glory hallelujah.
> Glory, glory, glory, hallelujah

It was late at night when they returned home, but their souls had been revived, their spirits were high, they were noways tired—and they saw that colored people could build their own church. They sang most of the way back in their boats, but by the time they climbed in their carts, the children and women all fell asleep immediately. Indeed, the drivers often dozed off too, leaving the horses to find their own way home. The horses, happy to be trotting on the road after being tied up in the woods all day, fell into a lively gait as they whisked the exhausted saints down the winding road.

After worshiping and studying with his brothers in Christ in the Petersburg Church for a few years, Abraham had another vision in which the Lord told him he was ready to establish his church. This time God called Abraham as clearly as he had in his first vision. When Abraham looked up into that glow of light that shone roundabout and all through him, God was holding the brown leather pouch that had been passed down from Abraham's great-grandfather. God handed the pouch to Abraham, who took it hesitatingly.

"Open it," God commanded, placing His hand on Abraham's shoulder.

Abraham did as he was told and took out a Bible.

"That is the Word that you are called to preach," God commanded.

Abraham started to leave with his Bible, but the Lord placed his hand on his shoulder. "Pick up your pouch and see what else is there," he thundered.

Abraham opened the pouch again and took out a hymnal.

"Lead your congregation in singing praises to the Lord," God commanded.

Abraham took his hymnal and put it under his arm with his Bible and again started to leave, but for the third time, God laid a heavy and majestic hand on his shoulder, and commanded, "Open your pouch again."

Abraham did so. Nothing else there. He looked up beseechingly at God, but God obviously awaited his removal of a third item from the pouch. Abraham searched every section and cavity and segment of the pouch. He even started to check inside the lining. And then he felt something cold—a key.

"That is the key to the church that you will build to read my Word and sing my praises," said the Lord, pointing to a church that had suddenly appeared in the vacant grove about a mile from Abraham's house.

This time Abraham would not hide the Lord's House in the woods. Rather, he prepared to set it out on the road for all to see, as the Lord had shown him. He went to the Courthouse and promptly transferred an acre of his land to the Elam Baptist Church, the acre that included the grove where the church appeared in his vision. All his friends in Freetown helped to build their new house of God, an exact replica of the one the Lord had shown Abraham. In years to come, visitors would comment on the rather elaborate interior, but this, too, was the master carpenter's expression of the Master's model. The pulpit rose up three levels. Behind it were three circular windows. One level below the pulpit was the Lord's table. In the center of the church, an elaborate chandelier hung from the ceiling. To the left was a piano. Seats on either side of the church encircled the first two levels.

When they finished, Elam Church was exactly like the edifice that God had revealed to Abraham. Abraham looked at the work that he and his brethren had wrought, and he said, "That's good."

They opened their doors to the free Negroes and the slaves. A few Whites mumbled about those niggers setting up their own church, but others suggested that was a good way for them to spend their time—praising the Lord in plain view of everyone rather than plotting against their masters deep down in the woods.

Abraham went to the business meeting of The Baptist Church in Charles City and announced to them that he had established Elam and solicited their help in the establishment of Elam's worship services and the development of their constitution. He was surprised he was so well received. The minutes of the Baptist Church note, "Abraham Brown was invited to seats with us."

In October 1813, Abraham went as Elam's delegate to the Dover Baptist Association in Richmond. His letter was so well written, his church's organization so effective, his representation of his cause so eloquent that the Dover Association did not require Elam to be represented by a White person as they later required other Black churches. Unlike other Black churches, Elam had no White members. The Dover Association did stipulate that they have a White minister, however, and they appointed Elder William Clopton. He came to each Sunday meeting, sat in the most comfortable seat to be had, listened to the sermons by Abraham and other colored brothers, drew his one dollar, enjoyed a good dinner, and quietly sauntered back to his feudal home. He rarely undertook to preach a sermon, but whenever he did, he always preached from one text and only one, which was "Servants obey your masters."[3]

Life for Abraham and Suzanna continued to be full of anxiety, but they truly did put their trust in the Lord. They no longer talked about running away to the North. Every night they fell on their knees and thanked God for bringing them safely through another day. Every morning they fell on their knees and prayed that God would protect them during the day that was dawning.

The children began reaching adulthood.

---

3 These two sentences are taken almost verbatim from The History of Elam Baptist Church.

One son moved to the North and started living in the White world. The parents knew things would be easier for him, but they could not help feeling he had rejected them and all their line who had struggled to secure a little land and a house of God in their besieged Freetown. After he wrote and asked them not to say anything in their correspondence that would reveal his identification with colored people, they said their last prayer for him and never allowed his name to be mentioned again in their house.

Their oldest son married and built a home on Abraham's land. The second and third oldest daughters were being courted by some fine young men in the neighborhood. Abraham and Susanna started fantasizing about new sons-in-law and even grandbabies. Their youngest was now 13, and Susanna, in particular, longed to hold an infant in her arms again.

But, alas, the stomach that started swelling belonged to Polly, who, though the oldest daughter, had never had a gentleman to knock on their door asking if she could take company. Polly was old enough and pretty enough (indeed she was the most beautiful among their girls), but she had a haughty air that frightened off all the boys in the neighborhood. She never graced them with a welcoming smile or a friendly word if they tried to approach her at church or at a picnic. Worried that her eldest daughter would be an old maid, Susanna had often tried to coax her into being more sociable with the young men.

Polly only laughed and declared that when she saw a boy who was handsome and intelligent like daddy, she might be friendly, but she didn't have time for these silly, clumsy, dumb oafs around Freetown. Besides, why would it be so bad to be an old maid? Then she could stay home and take care of her parents in their old age.

"And you won't be able to manage without me," she laughed. "Because as youthful as you are now, my pretty mama, one of these days you'll be creeping around [and here she started impersonating a decrepit and bent old lady], can't see to find your glasses [dramatizing], can't get your spoon of broth to your mouth [more dramatization], can't bend down to tie your shoes [more imitation], can't get up after saying your prayer [more imitation], might even wet your bloomers."

As Polly jumped up and down like an old lady shocked and appalled at a burst of urine running down her leg, Susanna could take no more. As hard as she had tried to restrain herself, she burst out laughing and slapped playfully at Polly, "Get out of here, gal, with your crazy self before..."

Polly paused to give her a kiss and ran out of the room before the next playful swipe could reach its mark.

A similar kind of scene had played itself out every time Susanna tried to talk to Polly about her future. Polly would always turn their conversation into a joke, and eventually, she would have her mother laughing with her.

And now pretty Polly, haughty Polly, funny Polly, poor Polly was pregnant.

But who was the father?

CHAPTER EIGHT

POLLY

Born to be free, she controlled her stern parents, reduced the arrogant Virginia Aristocrat to a bumbling adolescent, and meditated with the protective Spirits.

Though Polly had ten siblings, she was still an only child. It was not possible that she could remember when there were no other brothers and sisters, when she was, in truth, the only child her parents had. By the time Polly was four, Abraham and Susanna had had three other children. In this ever-growing family that reached eleven in as many years, Polly remained the true individualist. It never occurred to her (or to anyone else in the family) that Polly could not have her way. She wasn't really arrogant or self-centered or overly demanding. No, she was usually sensitive, caring, generous. But when she decided something and gave you what the family came to call "The Look," no one considered questioning her. While all the other children fought over toys and pets, over books and a paper and pen, over places at the table, over slights given and received, no one ever reached a stage of fighting—or even arguing—with Polly. Child or adult—everyone yielded to Polly.

It was never Abraham and Susanna's intent to indulge one child over the others—and they certainly were not permissive parents, but they were always awed by this rare and eccentric first child of theirs.

Polly had originally been pampered by her great-grand-mother Elizabeth, who moved into Abraham's house the day their daughter was born and coddled her for one full year. Though Elizabeth died one day after Polly's first birthday, the child always claimed to remember her great-gran' and would often accurately and fully recount things they had done together.

When the day after her second birthday, Polly went into Elizabeth's room and curled up in her bed with the pink and white quilt Elizabeth had made, initiating a ritual that would last a lifetime, her parents were nonplussed. Something about her quiet, calm, sleeping figure prevented them from yelling at her, from insisting she eat, from dragging her away to bathe and dress her. They just looked at their daughter, felt her forehead to be sure she didn't have a fever, checked her breathing to be sure it was regular, felt her little heart to be sure it was beating normally. All of this was done with silence and care as if they already recognized they were in the presence of some kind of trance or meditation they could only regard with awesome respect.

Outside her room, they debated whether they should seek medical help, whether they should do something, anything, but each time they eased open the door to Elizabeth's room, their daughter's spiritual calm comforted them, and they felt powerless to intervene.

Polly seemed to plan her own life in a way that continually amazed her parents. She was beautiful and precocious, walking at nine months, talking at one year, already questioning everything and everyone around her. The day after her first day of solitude, she arose from Elizabeth's bed and refused her mother's breast—no period of weaning initiated by her parents for this one. Thereafter she would sleep only in Elizabeth's room. It had not occurred to her parents to have her sleep anywhere, but with them for at least another year, but with a new infant in their bed, they were a bit relieved at what they considered Polly's premature move. So again, they did not challenge their tiny monarch.

The years passed, and the family grew. Major and Samuel were put into the room next to Polly's when each turned three. When Patsy turned three, Susanna rocked her to sleep and then went in to lay her in Polly's bed. The six-year-old Polly, seeing her mother's intent, flashed "The Look" and declared in a quiet but authoritarian voice, "She can't sleep in here."

"Why not?" the shocked Susanna meekly inquired.

"This is my room," Polly said indulgently, jumping up to lead her mother out as if she were lost and had mistakenly wandered into the wrong room.

Susanna was so perplexed when she returned to her room with Patsy that she could hardly explain to Abraham what had happened. She couldn't, herself, comprehend why she had let her six-year-old child command her as she had.

Abraham was so perturbed that it crossed his mind it might be necessary to take a belt to Polly, thereby violating a practice distinguishing his family from others in the neighborhood who believed in the efficacy of spankings: "Spare the rod, spoil the child," was the axiom that guided their childrearing.

Abraham, Sr., on the other hand, had prohibited any beating of his children, insisting that only slaves were beaten and only brutes beat other human beings. He would never forget the first beating he witnessed... just after he had been indentured to Mr. Danzee.

The young Abraham had shivered as the poor slave girl, whose only sin was resisting the overseer's crude sexual advances, begged to be released from the post to which she was tied, pleading that she not be struck again, and promising that she would never disobey the overseer. The sound of the whip lashing her naked flesh cut into the soul of the young boy who ran up, yelling, "Stop, stop!" as he threw himself upon the overseer.

William Johnson, who had already had his fill, laughed at the ineffective gestures of the child and threatened to give him a taste of the whip if he ever interfered again. But both Johnson and Abraham knew that Mr. Danzee wouldn't take too lightly to having his mulatto son struck. Yelling a warning to the poor girl about what would happen to her if she disobeyed him again, Johnson strode off.

Abraham cut his eye at Johnson and ran to help release Harriet—for it was his beloved Harriet, a beautiful fourteen-year-old that had befriended the lonely boy and jokingly called him her boyfriend. He first attempted to help her cover her naked breasts, since, despite the fact that the blood flowed from the open wounds on her back, she seemed almost embarrassed to have her breast exposed to him. Recognizing that the blouse that the overseer had torn from her body was too tattered to conceal anything anymore, Abraham tried to wrap his own shirt around her, but the pain was too great for anything to touch her lacerated back. Help was desperately needed, but the frightened boy did not know what to do.

Abraham ran to get Aunt Hatty, the plantation healer. Then he looked on helplessly as Aunt Hatty gently washed Harriet's wounds with saltwater and wrapped her back in a bran poultice. By this time, the whimpering girl had mercifully fainted.

Harriet was never, thereafter, the joyful, carefree friend he had loved. She never joked with him anymore. She was a broken slave.

There were not a lot of whippings on Danzee's place— Abraham had never seen Danzee, himself, strike a slave— but Abraham had seen enough brutality from the over- seers to determine that no lash, whip, or even switch would strike a human being in a home over which he had domain. This lesson, he had adamantly passed on to his children.

Thus, not having a beating as an option, Abraham, Jr. went to Polly's room to reason with the child.

"Why don't you want your sister to share your room? We are a family. I share my room with your mother. Your brothers share their room. You should share your room with your sister."

"I'm sorry, Papa," Polly replied as if she truly empa- thized with her poor father and regretted that she could not grant his wishes. "There is no space for her here."

"No space?" Abraham queried, amazed. "You have a whole big bed in here. Surely, you know many whole fam- ilies sleep in such a bed."

"I have to leave space for Nana Liz," Polly replied in a

calm but decisive tone that suggested nothing more needed to be said on the subject.

Abraham left the room as dazed as his wife. He believed
that he should be more authoritative, that he and Susanna
should determine where their children would sleep—and
this was a room where five or six children could comfortably sleep. But he didn't have the energy tonight to argue
with a spirit child who had visitors from another world—
especially if that visitor were his grandmother Elizabeth.

He would put his foot down tomorrow.

Tomorrow never came, and no sibling ever shared Polly's room, though as the years passed, three and four of the
others slept in rooms together.

As bright and aware as Polly was, she seemed not to know
that she was bound by the restrictions of her race and her
gender—and this caused Abraham and Susanna the most
concern. They were forever fearful that dreadful conse-
quences might quash this child who would not accept that
there were any restrictions on what she did, what she said,
and where she went. She lived in a world that determined
that as a female of African descent, she was someone
whose free status was a threat and an inconvenience to a
society that regarded her as nobody, nothing, a nigger who
wasn't even contributing as a slave. As a proud descendant
of the Native Americans who originally roamed this land,
the British who claimed this land, and Africans who built
this land, Polly thought hers was the preeminent claim to
freedom.

Her sense of entitlement was only enhanced by the realization that all who saw her were awed by her breathtaking beauty. The smallest of the eleven after the others finished growing, she was a petite 5 foot 2. Her hair was long and shiny, as red as her Nana Liz's had been many years ago. When she felt like dressing up, she could fashion her hair in styles other women would futilely try to copy. Otherwise, she wore it in one long braid reaching to her waist. Her big, sparkling eyes, her tiny lips, her dimples, her smooth olive skin were the envy of any female who saw her—White or Black. Hers was a beauty enhanced by what would elsewhere be considered flaws: the little black mole over her lip, a hair out of place and fluttering in her eyes, a smudge on her cheek, a torn hem after her romp in the woods, her flushed cheeks after a race—all imperfections that defined the truly perfect beauty.

Polly was as wild as she was pretty. Unlike her sisters, she loved to run and frolic in the woods and around the lake behind their house. As tiny as she was, she could outrun her brothers until they were almost full grown. She could swim like a fish. There was nothing in nature that she feared. She would pick up a snake and play with it, while her sisters screamed and ran for shelter. She would climb a tree and rescue a stranded baby bird in a sagging nest. She would help a horse deliver its foal without blinking an eye.

And yet she was not merely a tomboy. She could sew garments that rivaled Elizabeth's—she readily learned to knit and crochet and would spend hours at these womanly tasks just as she would spend hours in the woods when the mood struck her.

Like Elizabeth, she loved to read, and, like her grand, as well, she read and spoke with a more refined speech than most of her neighbors. Abraham was always amazed at how much her speech reminded him of his grand-mother's... there was still a hint of a British accent.

Evidently, it was Polly's sophistication that had caught the attention of the governor and Mrs. Schuyler. He was no longer actually the governor, having recently complet-ed his term, but he was still graced with that title, a prac-tice he encouraged. Considering making a run for presi-dent as he was, he fancied it best to be known by some title that reflected his preparation for the highest position in the land. After all, two other Virginia governors had pre-ceded him to the White House.

The Schuylers hired Polly to help serve their most ex-clusive parties at Greenleigh Plantation, especially those attended by British or Northern visitors, where the hosts did not want constant reminders of their slaveholding sta-tus. Schuyler himself "deplored slavery" (his own words), but he couldn't run his plantation without slave labor. He much preferred, however, to be waited on by the pretty, refined mulatto girls from Freetown.

Polly and her cousins Ruth and Martha occasionally worked weekends at Greenleigh. Thus, she saw nothing out of the ordinary one evening when a messenger came to inform her that Governor Schuyler was going to have her picked up on the upcoming Friday afternoon. She was to stay overnight at Greenleigh and serve their guests on Friday and Saturday evenings.

Polly was waiting at the gate with her basket at her feet when the carriage arrived and was only moderately sur-prised to see it was the governor, himself, who had come for her. He invited her to sit in the seat beside him rather than climb back into the carriage.

Her mild surprise turned to anger, however, when the governor came to Rt. 5 and turned left instead of right, taking them away from Greenleigh.

"Where are you going?" she asked with such authority that Governor Schuyler was almost too surprised to calmly carry out his little ruse.

"I... I, uh, have to, uh, pick up some, uh, uh... friends who will be, uh, uh, visiting with... with, uh, us," he replied with less calm than he attempted.

Schuyler was one of the most eloquent speakers in the state, and here a mulatto girl had him stumbling over every word like a babbling idiot. He had been cowed by "The Look."

"Then I will get down and walk from here to Greenleigh," Polly replied with such finality that he almost halted his horses.

Composing himself, he declared that he wouldn't think of having her walk. "This will, uh, take just a... a... a few minutes."

Soon it was clear they were moving toward Williamsburg. Polly was more angry than afraid. *What was he up to?*

He soon stopped at an inn, and preparing to hand his team over to the boy whom he had summonsed for assistance, Governor Schuyler reached to help her down.

"I have no reason to dismount here," Polly peremptorily declared.

"But don't you want to see Williamsburg?" His tone was consciously designed to cajole. "We will walk about the town and, uh... uh... have d-d-dinner here."

"I have no intention of getting out of this gig!" Polly announced with a finality that made him fear he would only attract attention to himself if he continued his endeavors to tempt her out. Not only was the poor fellow he had summoned to take his carriage standing there staring, but others were beginning to pause and peer in their direction.

He stepped up to whisper in her ear: "Please just step inside. You may remain in the lobby until I finish my business if you wish. I, uh, uh, cannot afford to have a scene here, my d-d-dear."

"My *dear* governor, that is exactly what you will have if you do not take me back to my father's home immediately," Polly firmly commanded. "I warn you. Within ten seconds, I will begin to scream that I have been kidnapped."

The little fool didn't know that the authorities would do nothing with a former governor accused by a Negro. She didn't seem to know that he could kick her half-white ass out here in Williamsburg, and Lord knows what would happen to her.

These and other angry thoughts flashed through his mind, but he did not waste more than nine seconds before beginning to take definitive steps to prevent the vixen from embarrassing him here where he was so well known.

"As you wish," he smiled, jumping down to go around to the driver's side, and dismissing the boy with a small coin.

He gripped the reins tightly so that she could not see how his hands were trembling as he set back out on the road toward Greenleigh. He glanced over at the composed girl who had just made him feel like a rebuffed child, and he wrestled with mixed emotions of anger and desire. He could not but wonder at her formidable resolve and the power that seemed to emanate from this diminutive dynamo. Too bad she couldn't present a bill for him on the floor of the legislature. She'd have those old boys quaking. He smiled at the thought and felt her glance surreptitiously in his direction. He felt confident that someday he would share this little joke with her. But not now.

He attempted casual conversation about herself and her family, but she seemed unwilling to talk to him. Flattery won only a cut-eye. Appeals simply made her stiffen in the far corner of the carriage. Finally, he apologized for anything he might have done that had offended her and begged her to tell him what he could do to make amends.

To this, she did respond. "I admire *honesty*," she declared as if she were the Queen of England. A pregnant pause and she continued, "I too apologize if I have not shown the proper respect to someone of your status, but I cannot help but feel that you have not behaved appropriately toward me. I consider it unseemly for an old, White, married man of your high status to entertain such thoughts about a colored girl as you obviously had in mind today."

"Old! *Old*!" he sputtered, unable to get beyond this first disqualifier to all the others.

She laughed.

He laughed.

For the first time, he did not feel that she was waiting to lower the guillotine upon his neck.

"I'm only *thirty-five*, you know," he began to explain, having been relaxed and released by their little joke, the gist of which was still causing him much concern. Age was never the obstacle that he thought he would have to surmount in his efforts to seduce this charming girl.

There was a pause, just enough to make him squirm. And then she laughed again. "Men are such incomprehensible creatures," she chuckled, "but I should not speak this way to you. I'm often careless of what I say, and thus, perhaps I should say nothing else to you lest I insult you."

"No, please, he interrupted, say anything you wish to

me... *Anything*! I shall never attempt to reprimand you .. despite your *youth*," he added satirically.

She laughed, allowed him enough of a pause to squirm a bit more, and then added, "I'm twenty-five—not so very young. Indeed, I'm considered something of an old maid by my family."

"Don't let them marry you off. There's no one here who is deserving of you."

Polly did not respond.

Her heart was racing madly, and her mind was cluttered with a sea of unsettling thoughts, but her lips were clenched as tightly as her little hands.

He hated to have their tête-à-tête end here, but he was fully aware of some boundaries that had been established. He would not give up. He wanted her even more now; however, he knew that she would not be won easily. He smiled thinking of the irony that he, the scion of one of Virginia's oldest and most respected families, he, who had had a chamber of Virginia's most powerful White males quaking at his command in the legislature, was now practically groveling before a Negra girl that he couldn't even speak to in the street. Indeed, right now, he would fall down on his knees at her feet if she would laugh with him again the way they had when she called him an old White man. For the time being, he reveled in the companionable silence that engulfed them. Night softly and slowly enveloped them. Mild September breezes kissed their cheeks.

It was outrageous that he should be feeling such excitement about "winning" Polly, but for the time being, he wasn't a powerful governor, and she wasn't a Negra wench. He wasn't even the horny aristocrat that set out that evening to get a little taste of nigger poontang. He was a man smitten with a desirable woman, still possessed by passion, but, now, even more, subjugated in caring. And he meant to win her on her terms.

But you've read the previous chapter, and you know she was won—if that is the word. Perhaps he pursued her until he was caught. Perhaps there was no victor and no prey here. No one ever knew the details of his pursuit and the consummation of their relationship, for Polly never offered this information... and who was there who would dare inquire?

And now, Abraham and Susanna were angrily demanding information from Polly.

She had not yet responded to any of their queries, her expression making it clear that they would have to calm down and talk intelligently rather than hysterically. She always made them feel she was the rational adult, and they... the children.

Abraham, still incensed, declared, "Well if it's not someone who's going to marry you, we better send for Aunt Liza now."

"Oh, no, *no*!" Susanna cried. "That's too *dangerous*!"

Polly, who had not deigned to contribute anything to the "discussion" thus far, promptly disabused her father of this thought without pause. "I will have my baby," she declared.

"Your baby! *Your* baby!" he screamed. "You don't conceive a baby by yourself. Who is the father?"

Polly's stern look was a clear reprimand. He hated it that he knew what it meant and was going to capitulate. In a calm and rational voice, trying hard to keep any sarcasm out of his tone, he entreated, "Polly, I'm begging you to tell me. Who is the father of the baby you're going to have?"

"I will tell you only if you swear by God not to confront him, not to interfere in... *any... way*. This is between the two of us and I... will... *never* tell you unless you both swear... on the Bible... that you will not take any *action—any action... of... any...* kind. You must also swear you will never tell anyone else who the father is."

The parents argued and resisted, but they knew that after twenty-five years of acceding to Polly, they would on this point too. Finally, they brought out the Bible and made the promise she required.

Two pairs of eager eyes sought to become one with their daughter's. Waiting... A short pause that seemed an eternity.

"Governor Schuyler."

Polly turned and walked calmly into her room, looking back sympathetically at her shocked parents and then softly closing the door.

Abraham and Susanna talked long into the night. Their hearts were broken. Abraham wanted to break his promise and confront the scoundrel, but Susanna declared that they had raised their child, to be honest, and they must now keep their vow to her.

They talked and talked about what was to be done. How to protect their daughter? What to tell the family? Finally, Susanna dropped to her knees to take her burdens to the Lord:

Is me, Lord, same old sinner coming to you again for help with my children. This time it's the cream of my crop, Lord, my first-born, my chosen one. Lord, she has drifted, drifted. Why, Lord, why? Why, no matter how yuh plant and feed and nourish, a foul breeze comes along and blows down your carefully tilled crop?... What am I to do?... Send a sign, Lord. Help this weary mother to lead her lost child back to the righteous path.

Susanna sighed painfully and slowly clambered back onto her side of the bed.

The night waned.

She and Abraham lay there wide awake, each with his own private reflections. Susanna, her thoughts moving to consider the child that would be born, touched her husband gently: "Abraham, what do you call the colored child of a Virginia governor?"

His response was quick and bitter. "A bastard."

In later years when Polly conceived her third child, Susanna would ask her husband, this time half-jokingly, "Well, Abraham, what do you call the colored child of a United States president?"

A melancholy smile crossed his lips. "Another bastard."

AUTHOR'S NOTE

Polly had three children, all of whom remained in Charles City, Virginia, married, and had children. The two boys bought land from the man reputed to be their father and lived until their death on that land, which adjoined his own plantation. I have discovered no record that Polly ever married. She continued to live on land she inherited from her grandmother and her father, occasionally selling small portions of it. The last record of Polly is in the 1870 Census, where she is listed as being seventy years old. Her brother and one of her sons were among the earliest Negro officeholders in Charles City.

ABOUT THE AUTHOR

Daryl Cumber Dance, Professor Emerita, Virginia Commonwealth University and University of Richmond, is the author of the following books:

Shuckin' and Jivin': Folklore from Contemporary Black Americans (Bloomington, Indiana: Indiana University Press, 1978).

Folklore from Contemporary Jamaicans (Knoxville: University of Tennessee Press, 1985).

Long Gone: The Mecklenburg Six and the Theme of Escape in Black Folklore (Knoxville: University of Tennessee Press, 1987).

Fifty Caribbean Writers: A Bio-Bibliographical and Critical Sourcebook (Westport, Connecticut: Greenwood Press, 1986).

New World Adams: Conversations with Contemporary West Indian Writers (Leeds, England: Peepal Tree Books, 1992). Second edition published in 2008.

Honey, Hush! An Anthology of African American Women's Humor (New York: W. W. Norton & Company, 1998).

The Lineage of Abraham: The Biography of a Free Black Family in Charles City, VA, 1999. Self-published. New and expanded edition with Daryl Lynn Dance in 2020.

From My People: 400 Years of African American Folklore (New York: W. W. Norton Company, 2002).

In Search of Annie Drew, the Mother and Muse of Jamaica Kincaid (Charlottesville: University of Virginia Press, 2016).

Till Death Us Did Part: A Story of Four Widows, 2020.